Acknowledgments

Thank you first and foremost to my husband Sam who has supported me in my writings since those tentative beginnings and my children, Farah and Ben, whose feedback has always been honest and true.

For her absolute belief in me and for her wise advice, I thank my lovely sister Jean James.

To the Lisburn Arts Advisory Committee and the Island Arts Centre for their generous help and encouragement over the years which has been much appreciated.

A number of the stories included in this collection have received awards and acknowledgments are due to Downtown Radio and Easons bookshop (Any Ordinary Day/Some Other Love), Maxwel Writers Week (Mattress Man), and the Mencap short story competition (The Chapel Field).

Thanks also to The Incubator Journal and North West Words for including my stories in their publications. All of the autobiographical stories have been broadcast on BBC Radio Ulster's 'My Story' series and special mention should be given to the producer Pauline Currie for her patience and understanding and for including 'Two Minute Timer' in the BBC anthology.

To my writing class – thank you from the bottom of my heart for your friendship, good humour and kindnesses to me even when I've been cracking the whip. You know who you are.

My gratitude and affection go to Eileen Casey and Louisa Goss for our sustained closeness despite the miles between us.

And finally to David and Jackie Stokes who have given me the encouragement to keep writing and have offered me this opportunity to share my stories with a wider audience.

Under a Cold White Moon

by
Lynda E Tavakoli

DAVID J
PUBLISHING

Contents

An Introduction...

I have written a couple of novels, tried my hand at scribing a play and composed an innumerable number of poems, but inevitably it is the genre of the short story that calls me back.

For it is in the short story that I can rid myself of those writing inhibitions that often restrain me in other genres. Nowhere else am I able to access quite so well the hidden part of me that secretly yearns to be murderer, mistress, bully or a child again – hypothetically, of course!

When I began to write short stories it was with a freedom that I soon found was addictive. The suspension of truth and the creation of characters that had thoughts and feelings I could only identify with in my imagination came as a kind of epiphany.

More and more I was drawn to subject matter that was uncomfortable and sometimes painful to confront but nonetheless offered tremendous opportunity to examine the human condition in all its frailty and flaws.

The characters included in these stories are purely fictional and any similarity to real people is obviously entirely accidental.

An Appropriate
Act of Love

I **WAS NOT A QUIET CHILD,** I'm told, the penalty for being the youngest of seven children necessitating a degree of forthrightness on my part, but still my candour did little to gain my mother's attention. I was, in short, her nonentity. And so it happened that from the age of five or six I set out to find a way through the seemingly impenetrable wall of her indifference.

From the vantage point of a high stool I'd often watch the back of mother's head while she stood at work by our kitchen sink, black curls springing erratically up and down the contour of her neck while the froth of dishwater fizzed between her fingers.

I couldn't say if she was beautiful then (although she probably was, I think now) but she had that look of someone long ago frayed around her edges. Such detachedness was a source of fascination to many, I imagine, but to a child it begot only frustration and annoyance; emotions that like some virulent staphylococcus virus seemed to invade my own psyche from a very early age.

My mother's eyes were as grey as the dawning of a flat Irish day, and emotionless to all her children, but especially to me. It was because I was her final straw, her last sprog to contaminate an already worn-out womb and by virtue of that fact I suppose, I became her nemesis. Something I accepted with begrudging antagonism.

"Stuart," she'd snarl through some invisible mouth in the back of her head. "Get on with your effing homework," or "Stuart, get up them stairs and tidy up that shithole you call a bedroom," and on and on without ever bothering to screw her neck round far enough to have eye contact with me, that final straw of hers. It was a verbal, grossly immature game she played, with me responding in kind and inevitably ending the loser to her far superior source of colourful language.

On the day of 'the event' as it later became known, my father had abandoned his fractious offspring to their regular after-meal skirmishes and escaped with the daily paper to the lavatory. Inevitably my mother wasted little time and like some dummiless ventriloquist embarked upon her favourite sport of Stuart-baiting in her husband's absence.

"Stuart, fetch that drying cloth right now or I'll scalp the legs off you," she threatened just as the crust I was sucking on was finding itself momentarily lodged in the vicinity of my larynx.

Fearful of spluttering breaded spit over my siblings and like a trout cautious of some wriggling underwater ambush, I closed my mouth and coughed the offending irritation slowly back towards my waiting stomach. My attention, however, remained on the agitated stiffening of my mother's shoulders as she waited for a retort that for the first time did not come and it was at that moment I knew I had her.

As her head rotated the full one hundred and eighty degrees it needed to fix me in her sights I felt the slow grind of teeth as my jaw clamped shut. This was a game I had won before even I knew the rules and if it had an aim then, the final outcome had surely been achieved at the very beginning. Suddenly I had my mother's complete attention without speaking so much as a single word.

"What did you say?" She hurled the words over at me across the linoleum, her denial at my silence oddly touching and unexpected. "What did you fucking say?"

My mouth smiled the smile of an obdurate clam sealing in words that might earlier have shrieked their way out but trapped inside my head their muteness confirmed my sudden authority. I had unwittingly discovered something wonderful; that the power of silence was infinitely more effective than the power of speech and even at that early stage of the game I knew that it was probably too late for turning back. So there you have it - the beginning. In the kitchen of an ordinary house in some common or garden council estate I was then to become an extraordinary boy.

When, after a fortnight of insults, bribes and finally serious personal threats to my well-being no one had elicited a single murmur from my lips, my mother dragged me mutely to the doctor.

"He won't talk doctor," she told him while systematically stabbing me in the shoulders with a stiletto-pointed forefinger. Then angrily to me, "Will you?"

He asked me to open my mouth for examination and I readily obliged. In truth it was a relief to finally allow even some of the unspoken words to escape albeit noiselessly into the air for it had started to seem like they had begun to clog up my mind. You have the control they were saying, as long as you can keep them in. But it was hard in those early days when at six years old it would have been easier to renege than not. Had it not been for the doctor's slightly patronising response that day I think I may have succumbed to the pressure to co-operate but as it was he merely confirmed a diagnosis I had made myself.

"Mrs Chapman, there is nothing physically wrong with your son," he told my mother, smiling. "This is a power thing. Stuart has embarked upon a game with you and right now he's winning it hands down."

My feet suddenly lost contact with the floor as I found myself hauled from the surgery and I never saw the offending doctor again. Later I would hear my mother saying to our next door neighbour, "Fucking doctors, they think they know it all."

At school the other children regarded me at first, with not some small degree of suspicion. After all, my behaviour attracted the undivided attention of a great many adults but this ultimately stood in my favour because it often detracted from the misdemeanours of others.

Consequently I departed primary school with an overflow of friendships for all the wrong reasons and even those had not been verbally consummated.

15

Meanwhile at home, the siblings who had stuck it out had come to accept my strange behaviour over time, treating me with embarrassed indifference that served only to fuel my mother's on-going frustrations. In the end she had been forced to seek help from the professionals for my 'condition' as she called it, when my father told her in front of me (it was always a source of amazement to me that because I wouldn't speak he also thought I couldn't hear), that "Stuart needed help because he was obviously a bloody retard and people at work had started to talk."

I felt the indignant objections hammering against my skull in an attempted break out and nearly relented then but he patted my head like I was the family pet and disappeared off to watch the match on telly. It was as close as I ever came to losing control.

But if my father had a casual attitude towards his seemingly retarded son then the same could not be said of his wife. Increasingly trapped inside her continued resentment she became ever more desperate to assert her authority and dragged me from one specialist to another.

"Stuart has a psychological disorder affecting his cognitive abilities," said one.

"Stuart suffers from a condition not unlike autism and needs very specific emotional support," offered another.

And, "I'm very sorry, Mrs Chapman, but your son needs a course of medication to help remedy his obviously complicated mental problems."

But the one I most enjoyed, "Stuart is a little shit whose fucking case I intend to crack before I die." This last always from my mother on the way home from every futile appointment.

By the time I left school at sixteen the specialists had all but given up on me, having devoted a decade to probing my subconscious without success. I was disappointed, my mother now remaining the only adversary to play the game out with, but it changed nothing at home. Or perhaps it did.

One evening my father failed to return from work. The house had been, as usual, quiet during the day, my elder siblings having by then dispersed to lead more normal lives elsewhere and I now wonder how I never noticed their leaving or indeed how long it had been since I was the only child remaining. The food was on the table; bacon, sausages, tomatoes, potato bread and two eggs – all fried as he liked it and now coagulating on my dad's plate. Mother sat across from me at the table, hands tidily on her lap; mine stuffed in the pocket of my sweatshirt making bigger the hole already there.

"Where is he?"

For an hour, maybe two, we sat like dead fish frozen into an icy lake and still he did not come. Beyond the window of the kitchen light was being sucked slowly out of the day and finally the grey gloom of evening started to invade the room. A fear was beginning to gnaw at me and although my mother had moved not an inch during that time I regarded the subtle change in her manner with growing panic.The eyes that for so long had scorched her resentment into my soul had taken on the look of a hibernating tortoise reluctant to accept the onset of its awakening. They were dead eyes to match the dead words that finally slunk out from in between her teeth,

"Now are you happy?"

My father never did come back to his wife or to me. One of my sisters said afterwards that he could no longer play the gooseberry in his marriage and I asked her, on a piece of paper, what she meant. All she did was to tear it up and slap me hard across the face, while seeping through the walls of the next room I could hear my mother's breath like an old clock ticking out the remainder of its time.

She won the game in the end, of course, as I always guessed that she would. The mystery to me was how it had taken so long for her to figure the solution out. From then on she never spoke to me again and right up until her death some years later the silent retribution she exacted upon me was fitting to my crime finally proving her worth as an adversary after all.

When I returned to our wordless house after the funeral I knew that this last silence would probably see the end of me too for after all there was no sport in continuing to play the game on my own. Earlier that same day one of the family had been clearing out the kitchen drawers and cupboards unearthing a deluge of obsolete paperwork that lay discarded in a corner waiting for final eviction to the bin. Among the pile was a dog-eared, faded blue file with my name scribbled across the front in mother's childish handwriting and curious, I had picked it up. Inside, carefully organised by date, were several hundred official documents concerning my case including appointment letters and professional correspondences offering varied and diverse diagnoses on my condition.

It was in some ways touching how she'd kept those indictments for all that time and I store them now inside a box in her room where these days I seem to spend most of my time.

The letters are a comfort in this soundless world of mine and sometimes I will take them out just to smell her soaped fingers lingering there with the memory of her touch. But every now and then you might find me press my lips to the paper secretly whispering my regrets in a voice gravelled from lack of use, the sound strangely hostile to my ears. In a funny sort of way I suppose, I owe her that much.

The Chapel Field

SOME CALLED IT COLD ACRE. OTHERS simply, the fallow. Yet I knew it always as the chapel field although neither church nor chapel was in evidence there during my lifetime at least. However, by the time my parents built a house on its strangely rich loamed soil, myth and imagination had combined to cement its mystical reputation firmly into the psyche of the local populace. But my father had been blessed with a sense of humour. He named the house 'Cold Acre Fallow' and my normally unflappable mother was suitably incensed.

"You'll only manage to annoy them, William," she said, eying him at the hearth where, poker in hand, he was sizzling the black letters into a flattened slice of bog oak. "They'll think we're taking the mick." Then seemingly as an afterthought, "It might bring bad luck."

I was sitting at my father's stockinged feet absently poking the stray embers under the grate and tipped my head slightly in order to see better his reaction to her rebuke. The corners of his lips remained curled pleasantly upwards. Those robin's eggs eyes of his never left the white-orange tip of the poker while he added the final 'w' to the sign and paused to survey his handiwork. I could still hear him whistling a jig when he went to hammer it in on the gatepost some moments later.

If the neighbours were annoyed by it they never said. Perhaps they had already accustomed themselves to the smiling demeanor of a man whom they had known from a cub and whose only misfortune was to be handed down a piece of dubious ground by his crabit and not so affable father. And so there was a certain forbearance bestowed upon my family by the community and none of the bad luck my mother had anticipated seeped into the pages of our lives. For a while at least.

Life on the Acre and its craggier appendages was as hard and as easy as for any of our fellow neighbours. Unforgiving winters bleached the countryside in swathes of snow on a bad year, yet mellow summers tucked their way in behind disappointing springs on a good one painting a landscape of unforgettable azure and green. It was on one such summer; the summer that I turned ten and was one day returning across the Acre from school, that I experienced my first vision. I say vision, but in truth it was more a sense of something harbouring the space between me and my sister as we progressed towards the house.

"Do you feel anything?" I inquired of my infinitely more sophisticated sibling when the sensation became so intense that I could no longer ignore its presence.

Her pace began to slacken and she turned her face deliberately to fix me with her hazel eyes. She possessed the same sunny disposition of our father and I was taken aback by the gradual furrow indenting her brow and an unexpected startled expression stretching over her face.

"You mean something spooky that sends shivers right up your spine?" she replied, "Like this?" And releasing both hands from the confines of her pockets she tickled her wriggly worm-like fingers along the contour of my back.

"That's not even funny," I said pulling away sharply when I realised how I'd been duped. "I did feel something."

"Whoooooh!" she howled, racing on ahead of me with arms flailing like a demented scarecrow and skinny legs kicking up dust as she went.

I waited until she had retreated behind an old yew tree near the corner of the house and could no longer hear her harmless mockery, before starting off again. But my feet had locked themselves into the ground as though the earth itself was somehow sucking me up and refusing to release its grip. Then quite unexpectedly a stab of pain shot through the back of my head – the part where adults are prone to patting you in church as you walk between the pews on a Sunday. A second it took, possibly less, I do not recall exactly now, but it indented itself like an unseen bruise within my skull. I was only ten years old; too young to understand it properly perhaps but even then I sensed that visitation rights of sorts had only just begun.

If she had died that day or maybe a week or two afterwards I might somehow have connected better the events, but she did not. Instead it was some eight months later that my sister met her death and by then all thoughts of apparitions or the like were long since absent from my mind. She had been with Dan in the stable; Dan, my father's gentle cob that never once was known to buck or shy or misbehave in any way, yet still he caught her with a hoof that saw her skull split clean from ear to ear. When I found her she was cold and motionless, slumped on the reddening straw and Dan was blowing warm breath pathetically into her lovely face.

My mother never really recovered from it and blamed herself in whatever way a mother could for the loss of a beloved and only daughter. Yet I knew better where culpability lay and agonized as to whether I should tell my parents of the part I played in their daughter's tragic demise. But what could I have said? That I had chosen to ignore a warning I myself had failed to fully comprehend? That I should somehow have foreseen my sister's death and thus prevented it? So it was that my confession remained unspoken until, albeit unintentionally, my father released me partly from my guilt.

Some months had passed since the funeral and we were out digging potato drills while the earth was still soft enough for spade and graip to take unchallenged. I noticed that the soil was changing in tone from a rich syrupy brown to pale honey every few yards and I remarked on it to my father. He seemed to chew the thought over carefully before making a reply, as though considering whether I was old enough yet to appreciate the value of his words.

"Do you believe the stories they tell about this field son?" he asked, an elbow leaning against the hilt of the spade as he paused in order to demand my full attention. I was wondering what his question had to do with the shifting hues of the soil.

"No father," I said, not knowing what else to say and unwilling anyway to tell the truth.

"This is the chapel field," he went on.

"Yes, I know that but there isn't a chapel."

"No son, but there used to be and long ago they say there was a graveyard here, right under our feet. In the places where the soil changes colour is the mark of a grave if you're inclined to believe it and that's where the stories have sprung up. They think we've built our house upon hallowed ground and disturbed the resting place of the dead."

He offered this like a teacher explaining some fundamental truth to an uninformed child, giving little hint of his own beliefs in the telling of it, but still I needed to know more.

"Do you believe it then, father?" I asked. "That there are ghosts here?"

He stooped suddenly and scraped a handful of soil from one of the drills letting the earth trickle through his blunt fingers before saying, "I believe that we can all give something back even in death." He drew the remaining soil to his nostrils and breathed it in deeply adding, "Even if it's just to feed a row of mangy old spuds."

I knew that he was thinking of my sister buried on consecrated ground behind the village church and it seemed odd that he should find solace in the thought of worms feeding from her corpse. Perhaps I was too young after all to recognise my father's wisdom and learn from his words but I was old enough to know that he had still evaded answering my question.

"And the ghosts?" I pressed. "Are they alive? Can they come back to punish us and haunt us from the dead?"

"If they think they have just cause for doing so, then yes," he said, "perhaps they do exist. But your sister is at peace now, son, and you don't need to fear any ghost of hers."

I could see that he misunderstood my meaning and was tempted to let it lie, for after all what purpose would it serve to burden him with childhood fantasies such as mine? Though stronger was my need for him to understand the inconceivable; my conviction that something within me had attracted the spirits of the dead which in turn had resulted in my sister's death.

"Father," I began, but it was useless; the words restricted by a terrible tightening within my chest that suddenly precluded speech. Yet he himself appeared unseeing to my pain, the space between us having succumbed to a force so bizarre that I alone could realise its significance and know then with sickening certainty that my father's fate, like my sister's before him, had already been sealed.

Within a year he was dead, felled by a massive heart attack whilst digging turf on the high bog not a mile from his beloved home. My mother had sent me out with tea and farls to dampen the hunger of his labours but his soul had already flown when I arrived where he fell, his big hand still clutching defiantly onto the butt of the spade. There was no surprise in it.

I had known, of course, it was inevitable and with equal conviction recognised the futility of my preventing it. For an impotence was seeping through my bones and with it the spirits of the dead whose graves, I was convinced, we had unwittingly defiled.

I began to notice other things too. A bird with a broken wing found some days after I sensed a baffling ache in my arm or a sightless rabbit, eyes sticky with some deadly virus discovered only weeks following an infection in my own eyes. Coincidence perhaps but such incidents and many other more besides began to torture me because I could do nothing to assuage the victim's pain and halt their ultimate deaths. And all the while inside our soulless house my mother slowly shrank indifferently into grief, cocooned within some grim and tragic wasteland of her own until the day I saved her soul by sending her away.

So I came to accept the fate that had been chosen for me; the Acre had become my nemesis where no living thing was destined to survive its retribution save for me. Each blade of grass, each leaf, each tiny insect vanished over time, sucked inexorably into the blackened sterility of the land.

I was afraid to stay. Afraid to stay yet more terrified to leave because I knew the thing I feared the most would always hold me to the land; the thought that I might carry the curse along with me blighting those outside.

Now with each passing day I wait and yearn for death. The final reckoning it seems is yet to come but only when the Acre claims its ultimate reward and frees me from its spell.

I dream these days of golden celandine in bloom and buzzards circling overhead or blackened earth becoming softened to a brownish hue once more. For at my journey's end and I am gone, the land I've loved will surely breathe again and underneath this hallowed ground the souls of the disturbed must find some rest.

Yes, I am ready now to pay the price. So therefore let it be.

All You Need

FOOTFALL. MY FATHER'S FAVOURITE WORD. A word he said rested in your mouth like a snowflake, dissolving its taste onto the tongue before speech. "We heard your footfall on the porch," he would tell me proudly on my calling days. "We feel the softness of you when you come to the door."

He wrote poetry. Sad, sweet, sometimes unforgivably sentimental poetry about his life, loves and his wife but I learned more about my parents through reading these than at any other time during the fifty years of being their daughter.

"That father of yours is such a romantic," my mother used to say with the smile that was forever dancing around the edges of her mouth. The smile that in profile became her miserable or cheerful face as the result of the stroke she was felled by eight years earlier. We made a game of it, laughing as she swivelled her head from side to side; sad face/happy face/sad face. But really there was only one face that mattered and that was the one that was screaming underneath.

I can't say that it should have been much of a surprise when the subject eventually came up. Death had never been an uncomfortable issue within the family as my father, a scientist by profession, allowed himself a healthy cynicism towards most things and my mother had simply always been, well, pragmatic. And it was something they passed it on to me, their ordinary nonchalance about their not so ordinary lives. For although the stroke had incapacitated his wife in ways that even he as her carer found difficult, it was only when his personal nemesis prolonged its visit that the real challenges began. The stealth of it shocked us all when finally we realised that my mother's misfortunes were but a bubble in the clots that conspired in my father's arteries and were furtively furring up his brain.

"You see the irony in this," he said to me one day when he could. "The same bastard is going to murder us both."

I tried to call in most afternoons after work when my father's day would welcome the sound of a human voice. Since the stroke my mother had been unable to produce a single intelligible word, something that had proved infinitely more challenging than the flaccid appendages that now greatly inhibited the dexterity of her movements. Any communication was therefore performed through the slow scratch of pencil on paper as her still sharp brain fought to make its presence continually felt. Yet my parents' lives were bound by an understanding beyond my own and its unravelling became the catalyst for what would eventually define us all.

I was used to seeing my father feed my mother, her snailed lettering having hours earlier suggested a menu for the meal. I had seen a spoon carefully enter the cave of her mouth and heard the slow slurp of liquidised food ingested into her throat and see again my father's big hand carefully wipe away dribbles with his thumb. So when I called in one lunch time unexpectedly and found my mother sitting alone at the table eyeing a plate of cold food I was, to say the least, worried. I found my father in the kitchen hunched over the sink, a white froth of bubbles popping between his fingers as he washed some dishes.

"Wasn't mama hungry then?" I asked when finally he became aware of my presence in the doorway.

"Who?"

"Don't be daft daddy. You know who." But he didn't. Not then anyway.

After that the periods of memory loss became like a train journey of unscheduled stops and starts, the track connecting the

26

stations shrinking with accelerated ease. Between them though, my parents somehow managed to be the two halves of a dysfunctional whole and life for them both seemed, to the outside world at least, sufferable. I had insisted on extra help from Social Services, a necessary intrusion which had been reluctantly accepted but without which would have made normal day to day living at home impossible.

A few months after the incident in the kitchen I arrived at the house with a present for my parents' fifty-fifth wedding anniversary. By then conversations with my father had become a kind of guessing game with me never quite knowing the person I might arrive to see. Most days it was the intelligent and articulate man who had nurtured and loved me all my life; the scientist-cum-poet with the big voice and even bigger heart. Sometimes not. On that day it was the former who greeted me, dunking down under the celebratory balloons dangling from the ceiling of the porch.

"Happy anniversary daddy," I said and kissed him on both cheeks.

"And what a wonderful day it is," he boomed, all smiles as though the sun had surprised the sky during a thunderstorm.

My mother was dressed in her favourite lavender blouse and coordinating purple skirt. She was sitting in a chair by the window so that the smiley side of her face was all I could see.

Slivers of silver shone through the usual dull greyness of her hair as if she had been earlier carefully preened and pampered. My father did not preamble.

"You're a good daughter," he said.

"Thank you."

"Your mother and I love you very much."

"I know that."

"So we know that you'll help us when we can't help ourselves." It was a statement I afterwards thought. There was no ambiguity of a question in his voice. "Your mother and I have made a pact."

It could not have been more clearly put and yet I struggled to take in the real implication of the words. The dryness that had suddenly claimed my mouth was precluding a response.

"We've had discussions," he went on. "These moments of clarity on my part are becoming less and less as you've witnessed but what we've decided was decided a long time ago, we want you to know that - even before you were born. It was always going to be a leaving of two souls together if it came to this." And there it was in all its starkness and eloquence - death by proxy.

"What is it that you're telling me?"

If I had for a second doubted their love, their devotion for each other, I would never have considered it. Their lives, after all, had been placed unconditionally in my hands and it was not something that could be borne lightly or without much searching of my own soul. As it was, I needed time to research the facts proffered to me outside of what I already knew which was that my parents' lives had become intolerable and it would only get worse.

"Dignitas," my father had said, "has denied us because of my own mental deterioration. You are our only hope. I'm sorry."

I am ashamed to say that for the few days after this revelation my thinking consisted of a single thought and that was the judgement of others. Helping one's loved ones to end their lives was surely the most heinous of crimes, punishable not only legally but in the eyes of whoever's god had an opinion. But in the end I could only hear my father's words telling me, without sentiment or self-pity, that they'd both had enough.

"How?" I asked once the decision was made.

"Here," he said.

The small stockpile of drugs was secreted behind probably the one place my father could remember to return to during lucid moments - his bulky and ancient radio. He had been accumulating the Class B drugs over the Internet for several months apparently since the refusal from Dignitas, and had been writing down quite matter-of-factly, what I should do. The timing would be up to my mother. She would choose a day when the signals to her husband's brain were failing to do much more than simply forgetting to feed her lunch. And there would be a sign; two circles pencilled on the notepad that remained permanently next to my mother's hand.

Two circles.

Just to be sure.

It was surprising how different everything seemed after the agreement. Even the folk from Social Services in their ignorance remarked at how relaxed my parents had suddenly become and it might have been easy then for me to renege. Yet I did not. Instead I read the detailed instructions I had been given - a sheet that ended with two names signed side by side with a kiss. For me or for each other, I wasn't entirely sure.

It was Good Friday and the rota for Social Services allowed for an early finish before I took over to oversee the remainder of the day. I exchanged pleasantries with the home help at the door and wondered had my parents heard me coming or had my footfall at last been consigned to a hazy poetic remembrance. They were in their bedroom, my father curled like a foetus on the side of the bed that faced my mother's reclining chair. She, in turn, was angled slightly backwards with an arm resting on the tray that lay across her lap, a pencil still upright between her fingers. They both had their eyes open.

I pressed my lips onto my mother's forehead and turned then to my father. Any remaining sharpness in his eyes had been diluted into their greyness and he stared dully past me as if I wasn't there. His cheek was cold to the touch when I kissed it and for a brief moment I hoped that he was already dead.

The notepad was resting at an angle beneath my mother's hand, the scratch scratch of her nail on the paper pleading for my attention although I knew what I would see before I looked. And they were there of course; two tiny circles almost touching and I wondered at the effort it had taken just for that.

"Mama," I said. "Are you sure?"

People will ask how I knew; how the certainty was unequivocal, and I can only say that for the first time in many long years I witnessed the gift my mother had freely given me throughout most of my life – a smile that lit up almost the whole of her face like a promise.

Following the instructions, I switched on the radio to their favoured Classical station and let the music play quietly in the background as I made up the medication. Then to lessen its bitter taste, I dipped my finger into honey and dabbed it onto their lips. I

29

gave the mixture to my mother first, placing a straw gently inside her mouth so that she could suck the liquid in herself and then I turned to rouse my father, helping to ready him on the edge of the bed. Neither of them gagged even though the experience could not have been pleasant to the senses and I waited until everything had been imbibed before leaving the room because that it was what they had asked.

There could be no nice ending to it. No twist of the tale to make the story okay. When I returned to the bedroom later both of their spirits had flown and I knew my father would have enjoyed the poetry in that. I sat for a while before making the phone call, afraid suddenly for myself but glad too, knowing that they would have done the same for me.

For love.

Only love.

Mattress Man

FROM THE ENTRANCE OF THE SUN-HOUSE Abdullah surveyed the aftermath of last evening's storm with resigned acceptance. The clean-up operation had added an hour to the beginning of his day but that was of little consequence to a man who had already dedicated twenty years of his life to a vocation. For in truth his work seemed not like work at all but more a continuing programme of learning in the habits and idiosyncrasies of the human condition. Abdullah ruminated unconsciously on his tongue and considered his good fortune knowing that he was indeed a very lucky man.

Every morning a white coat, freshly laundered and newly ironed, hung on a peg at the back of his locker door. Today he would inspect it with added scrutiny, ensuring that no particle of sand or dust dared invade the deep sanctuary of a crease in either pocket or cuff. After all Abdullah was nothing if not fastidious in his habits. He lifted the coat off the peg and ritually extended first one and then another arm inside a starched white sleeve thinking how soothing the fabric felt against his honeyed skin. So clean and unsullied. Clinical even. But he liked that – the fact that sometimes a guest mistook him for the hotel physician. The thought made his lips curl in satisfaction and the tip of a chewed tongue could be seen protruding from the corner of his mouth.

It was early yet. The sun had barely stolen a peek around the further reaches of the gardens but Abdullah set to his task with the determination of an ant bearing home the body of a dead comrade. No guest could be allowed to happen upon a pool that was anything less than perfect and in all his twenty years of dedication Abdullah had received not a single complaint. It was the mark of the man, everyone agreed – his patent attention to detail.

Fortunately the parasols, trussed up and secured the evening before, had remained impervious to the vagaries of wind and sand but many of the sun beds had succumbed to the force of the storm and lay upended like albino beetles kicking their legs futilely into empty air. The swimming pool, a corner of which was now serving as a receptacle for foreign bodies that bobbed hospitably together on the surface of the water, had also failed to escape unscathed. With his long hooked pole Abdullah retrieved the worst of the debris and as the first rays of sunshine seeped across the poolside he managed to complete his morning duties, surveying the results of his labours with a certain pride.

But Abdullah's uncharacteristic moment of contemplation was abruptly interrupted by the arrival of his first guest, a pretty Russian girl called Anya whom he had spoken with the previous day. He had been happy to accept her bribe of twenty dinar to secure a favoured place for the week and he had generously thrown in her mattress for free providing, of course, an additional tip was forthcoming when the sun went down.

Abdullah's powers of observation were legendary. He could spot an interloper at a hundred metres and with the skills of a jessed falcon would hone in on his prey with the same deadly precision.

Although weighted down with a cumbersome mattress or two his short staccatoed stride would immeasurably lengthen, followed predictably by a sideways dip of the head before arriving at his quarry to enquire deferentially, "You need mattress, yes?"

Given a negative response he would politely escort his charges to the outer regions of the gardens whilst apologising for the poolside places having been previously reserved. Only once had someone dissented by refusing to relocate their belongings and that exchange had buried itself deep into his subconscious with the intensity of a maggot feasting on a mango.

"Excuse please. You need mattress?" he had enquired politely at the time, seeing a man throw a towel on one of his most prized sun loungers.

A very white lady and a delicate-faced young girl with saffron curls stood by the parasol waiting.

"No need mattress," mimicked the man dismissively in reply.

"This sun bed not free, I sorry," Abdullah proffered, stepping forward slightly to obstruct the sun's rays and therefore have full cognizance of his detractor's face. He took in the man's red hair and ruddy complexion with a certain satisfaction knowing that before sunset his skin would be toasted nicely in the hundred degree heat.

Thinking about it now, Abdullah recalled proudly how easily he had defused the situation with a simple deferential bow before making a dignified retreat. It was an art he had perfected in order to appease his other more accommodating guests.

But today there were no such distractions and Abdullah put Anya in his most sanctified spot between the poolside bar and the hotel fountain. She smiled sweetly as he placed the mattress dutifully down upon the hard, plastic lounger and then attended to the position of the parasol. He imagined that he could feel her eyes scanning the back of his white coat as he walked away.

It was a busy morning. Thursdays were his most demanding days with the arrival of new guests but Abdullah did not object to the extra work providing he finished at precisely seven o' clock; a condition clearly stipulated within his contract of employment.

On leaving the young Russian he shuffled back to the sun-house for more mattresses but stopped abruptly by the open doorway to listen. It came faintly at first; the unmistakable timbre of a man's voice mixed with soft female laughter and through the crack above the hinges he could see their shadows moving rhythmically together in the half light of the locker room. There was no surprise in it, of course, as he had witnessed such trysts before and in more unusual places than his humble sun-house. They were commonplace amongst the wealthy hotel clientele but Abdullah had long since learned to hide his disdain, from common view at least, at such debauchery and now simply leaned against the doorframe to wait. Discretion would bring its own reward and later when they had gone and he fingered that crisp twenty dinar note in his pocket he couldn't resist a little smile.

It was a clammy day with leftover wisps of storm clouds threatening to occlude the sun in fits and starts and by six o' clock the guests had all but left the poolside. Abdullah began the task of collecting abandoned mattresses to scrutinise the fabric for misuse, but he sighed to think of how little respect people had anymore. And so, having secured the last mattress into its rightful place, he locked the door of the sun- house and left. He checked the time. It was four minutes to seven precisely.

Hurrying on along the winding pathways to the rear of the hotel he finally reached his destination and getting into his van drove through the shadowy bends and corners to the tradesman's entrance and on to the open highway. He maintained a watchful eye on the clock to ensure his arrival before seven-thirty. She would be waiting for his return.

At exactly twenty minutes past seven Abdullah opened the door to his isolated farmhouse and surveyed his worldly goods Everything was as it should be; neat and exact, the way it had been left earlier and he felt a satisfied smile settle at the corners of his lips.

The dark stone walls leaked their silence as he walked to the kitchen and selected a large knife from a drawer. He jammed its point into a crack between the floorboards and began to prize one up, his tongue jutting out between his teeth as he recalled his good fortune. It amazed him how easy it had been to entice her into his van that day when she strolled vulnerable and lost behind the hotel. He later discovered that no one noticed her missing for several hours afterwards and that someone thought they had spotted her playing in the sea earlier. Even after all these weeks they still expected her body to be washed up along the coast somewhere.

It had taken him many nights to finish it but eventually the hole he had dug was just large enough to fit one of his mattresses. He had specifically chosen the one her father had rejected which seemed somehow appropriate.

She lay on it now, tied up and gagged with only her eyes and nose exposed and her saffron curls sticking hotly to her delicate face. Soon he would prepare a meal for them; something exquisite that he would cook to perfection and serve on milk-white plates that had been scrutinised for their cleanliness.

He looked at his watch. Seven- thirty on the dot.

Yes, Abdullah was nothing if not fastidious.

All Made Up

NOBODY KNEW THE FRONTAGE OF HAROLD W Speers & Son Funeral Directors like Lydia Lamont. It sold its services in a manner befitting its trade with customary marble urn, plastic floral arrangements and gothic pledge of excellence dutifully displayed within the façade of an impressive, if rather outdated, oak panelled window. For Lydia visited her mother religiously every week in a journey of devotion that had seen her tread a familiar route from the city train terminal to the doors of the emporium many times over.

Alice, Lydia's mother, had succumbed to a disease that clogged her lungs some ten years earlier although it was a malady hard to fathom at the time given that Alice had never smoked a single cigarette in her entire life. Testimony to this Lydia always said, was the condition of her mother's skin on the day she died, possessing as it did a certain moleskin smoothness the envy of any prepubescent youth.

Though Alice had seen much hardship in her time, she had never been known to neglect her most significant asset; a natural if not timeless chic that she had in turn bestowed upon her only daughter, and Lydia would forever be duly indebted. But such perfection did not come without a price and neither woman would have considered risking public exposure without attending to their toilet at every available opportunity. Thus the Lamont legacy endured beyond the confines of the living after Alice passed away.

Lydia recalled clearly her mother's last wish on the day she died. She had been attending to Alice's pedicure, knowing that it was probably the last duty she would perform before death when she felt the feathery caress of fingertips rest upon her hair. Her eyes shifted their focus to her mother's lips as they mouthed three words she could not hear but instinctively understood, "Look after me."

"I promise, Mummy," Lydia had whispered in response, continuing to add the finishing touches of pink varnish to Alice's toenails before rigor mortis began to set in.

Other relatives were keen for the interment to take place immediately but Lydia was troubled. She had not been in any way satisfied with the cause of death proffered by the doctors and would not be deflected from seeking a second opinion. It was therefore necessary to plan for the body to be kept in cold storage until such times as proper funeral arrangements could be set in place. This had, in turn, resulted in the acquisition of the services of Harold W. Speers whose exemplary premises Lydia was now regarding from the vantage of a busy footpath.

Fixing a wayward strand of hair into place, her kholed eyes flicked one final glimpse at her reflection before she shimmied the remaining few feet to the entrance porch.

The delicate ting of a bell sang from above Lydia's head and she detected the soft suck of the door shutting fast behind her. After ten years it was almost like the beginning of a favourite melody and she knew exactly where the next notes would be coming from.

"How nice to see you, Miss Lamont," came the voice that would forever be a symphony to her ears. "It seems like a fine day outside. Was your journey pleasant?"

Harold Speers Junior stood where he always stood, behind a high mahogany counter towards the back of the shop where light from the window struggled to gain any significant ground. It had the effect of cutting the room in two and Lydia needed to advance several feet in order to take cognisance of Harold's face. She was always surprised by it. The deep-set hazel eyes and slightly crooked nose, the strong jaw that clicked occasionally when he spoke and that mouth; Lydia could not describe the mouth. Except perhaps to say that if there was ever a mouth made to be kissed, it was his. But the surprise in his face was held in his expressions that changed as often as shifting clouds proclaim the arrival of a coming storm. She found his expressions disarming but never in a disagreeable way and wondered why such a man had remained for so long a womanless man, for want of a better word.

Lydia's eyes finally found Harold's. "The train was slightly late I'm afraid," she said apologetically without unlocking her stare. "I do hope I haven't put you to any inconvenience because of it."

"None at all, Miss Lamont. None at all. In fact, your mother has only just arrived so let me show you in without further delay." Harold's slim hips slid between the gap in the counter and he indicated to a small door in the corner of the room where the words 'Chapel of Rest' were displayed in a discrete sign above the door frame. "Please," he said.

Harold was too much of a gentleman to interfere with a ritual that had been performed every Saturday for a decade. Yet there had certainly been a time at the very beginning when he and his now deceased father questioned the bizarre but entirely legal arrangements requested of them. A time, indeed, when their moral principles had been tested in the most stringent way, but in the end it was Lydia's filial devotion that won them over; nothing more or less.

In the intervening years Harold had witnessed her visits, week on week, month on month, and apart from that first day when certain health and safety regulations needed some explanation he had allowed her to enter the funeral parlour on her own. Afterwards when the visit was over and Lydia had gone he merely returned Alice to her place of rest within the refrigeration unit.

Lydia's hand was now twisting the handle of the door and she disappeared into the candle-glowed surroundings where her mother's body had been appropriately laid out. The room smelled of wax, church wax, not scented or overpowering or even for that matter, religious, but a smell if one could have it, of contentment.

Alice's coffin rested on wheeled plinths in the middle of the room. It was the fifth coffin she had occupied since her death and at a cost of near enough one thousand pounds per purchase Lydia felt she had undoubtedly earned that weekly hour of privacy with her mother. There had been other expenses too, of course, not least of all the fees she paid to Harold Speers and Son, but she begrudged none of it for she had made a promise and intended to honour it to the end.

Lydia approached the coffin and sat quickly down on the chair Harold had considerately provided for her on all her visits. Beside it was placed a small table, its cover a freshly laundered square of white muslin where she carefully placed the case she had been carrying from home. Only when it was opened and the contents fanned out in front of her did she finally turn her attention to Alice. Lydia marvelled at her mother's skin. Perhaps there had been some deterioration in texture, a little scaling of the surface yes, but nobody could say that Alice Lamont hadn't managed to age well in death.

"Hello mummy," said Lydia softly into the coffin, "I've come to look after you again like we agreed remember. What colour would you prefer today?" A candle stuttered in the corner and a soft rush of blood tingled through Lydia's fingers for a second or two. "Well now, there's a surprise," she said. "Pink again. But you'll have to be patient mummy. You know we have some small ablutions to attend to first."

Lydia lifted a pack of large cotton pads from the table and set to work. The task of refreshing padding in the stomach cavity was neither dignified nor terribly pleasant, but necessary. And she had become so practised at it that barely a few minutes were stolen out of their time together. When she had finished she turned her attention again to the remaining items on the table. Only yesterday had a nice lady at the cosmetics counter recommended a special brush instead of a sponge for using the foundation. "It gives much better coverage," the woman had explained, "And it saves a lot of money as you only use half the amount." It seemed to make great sense to Lydia who immediately purchased one brush for herself and another for her mother.

"We'll try this today and see how it works," she told Alice as she dipped the tip of her new implement into a pot of foundation and with the deftest of strokes began to flick the silky liquid across the stretched scaly outer covering on Alice's face. Little pieces of skin leached themselves onto the fine bristles of the brush but Lydia disposed of them discretely lest her mother feel subjected to any further loss of decorum.

"I'm so pleased I took her advice, Mummy," she was saying as she laid down the brush. "I do believe it creates an added depth to your look and I think you'll be very pleased with the result. Still, I'm disappointed that you want the pink for your lips again but never mind, you always know what suits you best."

Lydia unscrewed the top from a rather pricey looking glass pot to expose its glossy cerise innards. She allowed the sweet suggestion of raspberry to linger in her nostrils for a second or two before she drew her little finger along the gummy surface and carefully began to paint Alice's mouth.

The clock on the funeral parlour wall was showing ten to two when Lydia clicked the metal clasps into place and locked up her case. She was satisfied with her achievements and allowed a hand to settle on her mother's cheek in the final gesture of connection that always concluded their assignations.

"You will always be beautiful to me, Mummy," she whispered, "and I'll be back to see you again very soon."

She could sense Harold's presence in the other room, waiting as he always did, to escort her outside and she knew the time had come to take her leave.

The young Mr Speers was standing sentry by the funeral parlour door as it opened. On his face he carried the look of a man much perplexed by the woes of others and Lydia had, for as long as he could remember, been his favoured client. It had often struck him as odd that she never requested the second medical opinion so desperately sought when her mother died but over time he had come to accept her dalliance as eccentricity. Besides, she was quite, quite beautiful with the most sensuous mouth he had ever seen, and emerging now from the Chapel of Rest he could detect a faint trembling of her bottom lip.They had never touched but today Harold sensed her vulnerability more than ever and offered a hand in comfort as he escorted her towards the exit. Their fingers barely connected but each knew the significance of the gesture without the need for words and when Lydia re- emerged onto the pavement outside her heart sang in her chest.

The camera flashes assaulted her without warning, their jagged shards of brightness magnified by the reflection from the window, and an anonymous voice was shouting, "Does your mother look like a vampire yet, Miss Lamont? Is it true that her corpse has got no skin? Any comment, Miss Lamont? Miss Lamont, look this way!"

The reporter's words pierced Lydia's soul as surely as a dagger might have pierced her singing heart. Two perfectly manicured hands flew to cup her ears and muffle the vicious onslaught of words but she felt her legs suddenly weaken with the shock of discovery and stumbled out over the curb onto the busy road.

As her temple was connecting with the nearside tyre of the Number Sixteen bus the door of Harold's shop was sucking shut behind him outlawing the world outside. His feet took him towards the Chapel of Rest but his mind was filled only with a single thought; that longed for touch of Lydia's fingers against his own.

Over time he had come to recognise her weekly visits not as some macabre ritual but as a journey of the purest and most devoted kind of love reflected in those painstaking hours she spent making up her dead mother. Often, when he was returning Alice to the refrigeration unit after the visit, he would study Lydia's handiwork and admire the dexterity involved in decorating the decaying face of a ten year old corpse. At times he had been tempted almost to ask if he could observe the proceedings but professional to the last, had resisted the urge to impose upon another person's grief.

Now he took time to pause at the door of the parlour envisaging Lydia on her journey home, those smart peep-toe shoes clipping the footpath as she hurried to catch the train at the terminal, the immaculately coiffed hair that rarely shifted from its early morning styling, the merest glow of sweat daring to glisten above those artfully chiselled eyebrows. And he could even imagine hearing the gentle timbre of her voice abruptly cry out to him, words that sounded something implausible like, "Harold, please look after me." It was a fanciful, if not appealing notion but he knew she must be long away now and therefore directed his thoughts back to the reality of the present without further deliberation.

Alice remained inert within her coffin and Harold allowed himself a perfunctory peek inside before sealing the lid. Lydia, he observed enviously, had displayed yet again some extraordinary make-up skills with her mother and he made a mental note to offer his congratulations during her next visit. Then silently with the wheels beneath the plinths beginning to slide easily across the marble floor, Harold resumed the task of putting Alice back where she belonged.

Until the next time.

Once

I**T'S QUIET IN THIS PLACE.** All I hear are the bones of the dead whispering to me from the ruins of the poorhouse whose fallen gable wall I can see easily from where I sit. The elements have done their work across the years, gorging out the integrity between the bricks, eroding any history that has lain dormant in that now empty space of rooms; but that does not prevent me from remembering. No. Remembering has become my saviour and the lynchpin that protects my sanity, for the old (and I am indeed old now) are the lost of us and we, the lost, must cling to what we can in order to survive.

My mother brought me here when I was not much higher than her knee. The place was in the townland where she had been born and we were visiting, on foot, a poorly relative not long, I recall, for this world. We passed the old workhouse on the way, standing then as it is now, beside the banks of the Blackwater whose eddies sucked the brown darkness into itself as though needing to justify the name. The building had, even then, been derelict for some time although every wall was still intact and the roof saddled itself comfortably over any existing trusses.

When we stopped I could feel my mother's softness squeezing my palm, her heartbeat pulsing at the tips of her fingers, her love of me like blood, coursing its way from one of us to the other. I raised my chin to look up at her, waiting for her words patiently, for she was apt to think long before offering them up, and shortly the reward came in a way that I could not have then expected.

"Listen," she said, her lovely eyes fixed upon my own. "Listen to them talking to us, Dora. Can you hear?"

I listened, pressing my ears out towards the surrounding space as much to convince myself that I could share with her something I did not understand but all I could hear was the river's rush over rocks and a soft low of the cattle coming from a neighbouring field.

"No, Mama," I answered truthfully, knowing what she meant. "I don't hear anything".

She was standing now looking upwards toward the high row of windows that had long been blinded of glass and to the chimney that shocked its way through the beleaguered roof. Releasing the grip on my hand she pointed out towards them.

"I always wondered about the children," she told me, "and how they would have slept top and tail with one another squeezed in rows. We'd see them on our way to school looking down at us with their bare eyes."

I could not envisage my own mother of an age so young as to be going to school but I nodded anyway. It seemed important that I allow her simply to utter the words.

"Afterwards, when it closed, a lot of them were buried over there," she continued, nodding towards a thin copse of trees on the far bank of the river, "in Bully's Acre." And with that, from her mouth came such a sigh as could have saddened even a stone's heart. "Our family was never so poor as to not be able to look after each other," she added.

It is strange the things we choose to remember. And those things, too, that we decide to forget.

As I sit here now in this quiet, lonely place recalling my mother's words and looking out upon the ruined workhouse I feel the presence of those children so intensely it sends a shiver through my heart.

Perhaps it is the curse of old age to carry with you the burdens that you could not suffer as a child but there is no guilt to it, nor should there be. What was before has now become the present and foolishness lies only in failing to learn a lesson from the past. I hope I have the wit left in me still to believe it.

Today I wait in this new building that they like to call a 'home'. Although they built it near the original site it is as far from a workhouse as any place could ever be with its white-walled sterility and state of the art facilities for the elderly infirm. No one but me can know the irony of the circle I have travelled to arrive back here, but I take comfort in the memory of the in-between regardless of the regrets and sorrows on the way.

A car scrunches up on the gravel outside and I see that my own daughter has come to visit, something I treasure, although it is she who put me here. It was a deed done not with belligerence but with a genuine desire to do what was right, yet knowing this does not give either of us the comfort that it should. I ought to be at home where I can heal myself with the familiar, but I will not ask for it as a rebuttal will only pain us both.

She comes in smiling, but behind those green eyes is a look of abandonment impossible to conceal. It is not for herself but for me and I do not know how to respond to it except to welcome the warmth of her embrace as easily as I succoured her when she was a child.

The others here stare over and a woman nearby weeps suddenly without restraint, the white spit from her open mouth fizzing as it settles on the carpet near her feet. My daughter moves quickly with a tissue to mop up the mess, stroking the woman's hand as she moves away and I am touched by this small act of kindliness towards a stranger which was neither asked for nor expected. Then she returns to sit on the arm of my chair saying, "I hear they have a cat likes yours here, Mummy. They'll let you stroke it sometime, if that's what you'd like." But I don't like. It will only serve to make me miss my own Puss Puss more than I already do.

"It's okay," I lie, "I'm not that fond of cats really."

Through the window a sky of washed-out blue is troubled only by the smoky path of a jet stream. It triggers a memory of the Spitfire pilot who wooed me during the war; dashing and arrogant in equal measure and quite a catch for a farm girl such as me. Yet it was a sweeter, gentler and much poorer beau I eventually chose and the half century that we were wed somehow proved my judgement true.

"Let's take a walk outside, Mummy."

It's my daughter again, gathering up my belongings and taking my elbow to prise me from the chair. How tired these old bones have become from just the sitting and looking; but I do not resist. It will actually be a relief to feel air that has not been tainted by age like an overly- matured and vile smelling cheese, so I allow myself to be lead to my room and collect my coat.

At the main door we wait to be allowed out, another irony when I think of all the post-it notes the family stuck up around my own home. Bright orange and yellow stickers issuing little warnings such as: Don't forget to lock the door! Don't let anyone in mum unless you know them! Now they'd prefer that I just didn't escape.

The fresh air helps me to feel a bit more like myself. I enjoy the slow walk down past the workhouse (although I do not allow myself to look this time) and over the bridge to where there is a plaque hung rustily on an old gate. It reads: 'Bully's Acre. The burial place of the poor of the district - in memory of those within.' We have read those words many times, my daughter and I, but in truth every time is like the first for me and it is now almost too much for me to bear.

"I'm done," I say simply, squeezing my daughter's hand and feeling the warm pressure that returns it. I try not to show that I know she is crying. We walk on further until the silver birches shade out completely any rays of the diminishing sun and stop where the moss under our feet ensures that any footfall will remain undetected. I like the idea of it, this spongy bed where once they have softly fallen, those folk whose kin could not look after them.

"Can you hear them?" I ask, knowing by the look in my daughter's face that she does not.

No, she cannot hear the voices yet.

But she will.

She will.

In Articulo Mortis

I OPEN MY EYES AND SEE on the magnolia emulsioned wall opposite my bed, a clock telling me that it's six thirty-five. Dawn light or the dying rays of the sun seep through the curtain crack and come to rest near the hillocks of my feet underneath the blanket.

Night or day. Winter, autumn. Old and young. Everything is the same. Everything is everything and nothing at all.

This is my life. It exists now mainly inside this room yet here in this body and in this head there's another life. I don't speak often about it for I know there are few who still care, but if you're willing perhaps you might listen a little to the ramblings of an old man shortly before he dies. I've shocked you? Then I apologise, for it's not my intention to make anyone feel disturbed by my admissions, but time chases me and soon (perhaps even today) I'll have stood my ground and allowed it to offer its final embrace.

Is this what I do now? Breathe and wait. And in between remember things that were never important before and forget the ones that are significant now. Like when we sawed logs together, my daughter and I - the to and fro of the serrated metal jamming frustratingly because she kept losing the vital rhythm of the saw.

"Thanks for letting me, Daddy," she said afterwards, her eyes screwed up with the truth of an eight-year-old or twenty-eight-year old. Either way it's of no matter anymore and it's a wonder to me that I recall such an insignificant event at all.

Outside the lockless door with its stains and bruises telling their stories on the paint, life is rummaging around in the corridor. It reminds me of mice that holed up inside the wall cavities of my childhood; the busyness of their little rodent legs resonating through the plaster until the poison that my mother had set for them finally took effect. Then a week of skunky stink that accompanied their shrivelling bodies before the final disintegration into the ether. In here, behind these creamy walls, there are decomposing bodies too. No one believes me, of course, but my nostrils don't lie when they smell death which is just about every day.

She comes in without knocking. Her hair is fakely auburn, only half tied at the nape of her neck as if she'd lost interest before the exercise was complete. She doesn't smile much I remember and her name begins with a P - Paula, Pauline, Pamela or something. On the badge over her left breast she's identified as Patricia.

"Hello Patricia," I say. "Please come in."

But she ignores the sarcasm and heads straight for the window where the morning or evening light spills over my bed in great splashes as she pulls away the curtains.

"Good morning to you, Arthur," she says. "It's going to be a beautiful day." She's directing her gaze not at me but out beyond the glass to a field spreading its muddied furrows into the far distance. I wonder does she see what I have seen there; my father, his back stooped over the plough as though a knowledgeable wind supported him, and Dan, our horse, feathered legs straining with the puff and blow of exertion it takes for each channel to be deeply enough sliced."Yes," she says again. "It's going to be quite beautiful."

Her back is as straight as a silver birch, the shoulders of the green overall sitting level with each other but her head's tilted slightly to one side like my daughter's quirky pose in old photographs. Just for a second I wonder if it's actually her but then the woman, Patricia, turns.

"You're not like my daughter at all," I say.

It comes out like an accusation although I don't mean it to be and she looks straight at me, a sunbeam haloing her head.

"And I didn't claim to be Arthur," she says back matter-of-factly. "Now let's get you up and running, shall we?"

What do you think about being talked to like a child? What do you think I think about being talked to like a child? So I tell her, "Don't frigging talk to me like I'm some kind of retard."

I expect her to tighten up in the way caterpillars do when you try to lift them, or at least show a reaction that offers a small glimpse of what's really her. But her demeanour remains composed, and without the slightest hint of irony she tells me not to curse and to start behaving myself like a good boy. Not for the first time I notice that the colour of her eyes doesn't match the colour of her hair. It's confusing, don't you think? She shouldn't have black eyes with auburn hair - it just doesn't make any sense.

"Your hair's lovely," I say anyhow. The clock is telling me that seven minutes have passed since Patricia's unannounced arrival and I detect a fractional upturn at both sides of her mouth.

"You don't mean that, Arthur," she says. "Yesterday you said my hair looked like shit."

"Yesterday your hair was brown."

The smile stretches to show her teeth, the front two overlapping just enough for me to think her reasonably attractive. She could be twenty or fifty-five and she should be a lot thinner. Her backside is rounded and wobbles slightly when she moves but her breasts look like they've been recently encased in concrete. The combination does something to my brain (you must have guessed that) and an irrepressible desire splurges along these useless bones in waves. If she is aware of it, it doesn't show.

"My feet are not too happy," I tell her as she pulls down the quilt and folds it untidily over the end of the bed. Then she looks toward my feet and I wonder why I said something so ridiculous. I'm ashamed of the blue veins drinking their way over the scaly scurf of each foot; of the misshapen toes kissing their reluctant partners and especially I'm ashamed of the nails that are as bumpy and gnarled as the horns of a goat. You probably think they stink as well and you're probably right, but there's nothing I can do now to cover them up. So then she puts her hands inside the pockets of her overall and draws from each one a plastic glove.

"You could have been a magician," I say, impressed.

"Let's see these miserable appendages, then." She lifts my left foot with her two gloved hands, rotates it gently before doing the same with the other one. "No," she says, "definitely not too happy either of them, but I've seen worse. We'll sort it out later, but now you'll get me the sack unless you get your proper clothes on."

It takes a good fifteen minutes to toilet me, wash my every orifice and start preparing me for the coming day. If you don't know the difficulties of this then I imagine you are either young or have avoided contact with humans over the age of seventy. I hope you're beginning to see this now.

"Who are you talking to, Arthur? Half the time I can't hear a word you say."

She's got my arms above my head and is hauling off my pyjama top. I feel rather than see that my torso is the colour of watered milk.

"Nobody important," I say and mean it.

She chooses a clean shirt from the wardrobe and helps me put it on but has difficulty with the buttons because the plastic gloves are still sucking at her fingers like flaccid condoms. I wonder is she doing it on purpose. But before I can ask there is a soft knock from the doorway and a small child pokes her head in through the opening gap. I say small child but in truth I know this other girl has been here with me before helping the P woman out. She too wears an overall and she comes in shyly, her head tucked into her neck and her eyes towards the floor. I want her to lift them, to see her eyes and know that they suit her face because for some reason it really matters. She approaches the bed and makes the P woman jump.

"Jesus, I didn't hear you coming in there, Wendy. You're as quiet as a wee mouse."

I did tell you that they were out there didn't I? But I want this one to leave because her presence will now have made me invisible again. When it is just two of us then at least I can pretend I exist.

"He always tells me off when I'm too noisy, Patricia," says the interloper, her voice gravelled and low. "Sorry I'm late. It's my birthday and I was out on the town last night so my head's a bit delicate today."

"Happy birthday you," says P for Patricia. "How old?"

"Seventeen and God it feels ancient."

Then even though her eyes are still lowered, she seems to notice me and asks, "How old do you reckon he is?"

"I have a name," I point out, disgruntled, but this is ignored.

"Over ninety probably," Patricia says. "But he hasn't lost all his marbles yet."

"That's disgusting," says the child and shivers.

"I mean his mind, stupid. Now help me get him onto the chair and ready for breakfast."

For the first time I see the girl, Wendy's, eyes. They are the most unusual colour of bog-green with sparks of turquoise near the pupils. I'm reminded of a description I learned in school about the dark circular opening at the centre of the iris where light enters the eye. It seems prophetic somehow and although I don't wish to alarm you again, I must say that the momentary fixing of this child's gaze into mine has caused me the greatest elation. Don't ask me to explain it to you more than that for I'm unable.

Because there's not much left of me anymore and there are two of them now, I'm transferred quite easily from bed to wheelchair. In the time it's taken I've learned that Patricia's husband is away doing something undisclosed across the water, her children can't find work and are back living at home and she'll be heading off to her other job when she finishes this shift. Meanwhile Wendy's boyfriend treats her well, her mother is dead and she'll be starting further education when the summer ends. I want to tell them that I'll be dying soon, that the world can be a pile of crap only if you give it the chance and that there's a time to ask anybody's god who'd agree to it, to motion you away.

Now I'm in the chair and my feet feel happier having been freshly talced and socked up. I go to say thank you but what comes out is bound to sound like the someone who has lost his marbles who isn't me.

"My world is torn asunder," the marbleless person says. It sounds dramatic and archaic like words from Shakespeare or

Chaucer or somebody as old as Methuselah but I realise that it's coming from me in this room, right here at this very moment.

"What's that, Arthur?" asks the P person. "You're muttering again."

"He said his world is a sort of blunder," says the girl with the beautiful eyes whose black pupils dilate and contract as she moves about the room. "Arthur. Isn't that what you said? Tell Patricia."

I'm back to being visible again it seems.

"It doesn't matter," I whisper and start to cry, the tears stinging my cheeks and rolling into a fold in my neck, remaining there like droplets of dew that have formed within the well of a leaf. The girl lifts a tissue and soaks up the wetness as the older one turns her head away so that it's impossible to see her expression though I hear her say to the window and the field beyond. "He was so with it earlier too."

The clock is moving its big hand over the minutes but time is standing to attention now in the sudden stillness of the room. It's as if the trenches of the war have been transported to this spot and we've all been stunned by the sudden explosion of a mortar shell. Patricia's discomfort forces her to break the silence first.

"Arthur, you know that your wife's coming to visit today."

"I know." But who is this wife? Can you tell me?

"And she's bringing your grandchildren."

"Of course." Do you know that the lies they tell you in this place are terrible?

"Can you understand?" It must be the older one still talking because the child has disappeared from the room like a feather puffed away by a single breath.

"I need to see her," I say, desperate.

"I told you, she's coming later with the wee ones."

"Not her," I say, "Her," and I point my finger towards the opened door.

"Oh, you mean Wendy. She's gone to help with the others. Don't cry, it's upsetting me." I make a grab for her arm but only succeed in snatching the tips of her now gloveless fingers. She jumps back, suddenly frightened.

"Don't be doing that," she says, "it's not like you. Arthur, don't you remember all the things you've told me before about your family, your life?"

What a stupid person to think that I can go to that place again so easily but I make an enormous effort to try.

"You're very good to me," I say, "but I need her to come back. I need her eyes."

It's a clear thought, as clear as the sound of the Road Raider bell on my mother's old black bicycle, but the woman's face is showing a terrible disappointment or something else I'm failing to recognise. I know it's pointless to say anything else and there's a deep sigh before she speaks back.

"Right then, let's get you on down for breakfast."

So as the wheels of this chair revolve under me I can tell you now that it won't be long - the moment that frees me from this tortured life. For I've decided you see, and when I find her eyes and wither into the blessings of those dark holes, it'll be soon.

Soon.

Taken

THEY CAME AND FILCHED AWAY HER belongings one blue-skied morning in the middle of a July heat wave. She had been dead and buried a year by then but no matter; like a fine wine the remains of her lost life seemed only to have matured in significance with the passing of time.

I was not so bitter about the other things, for they had taken much more than the meagre offerings of an out-dated dressing table, but their lack of discrimination ignited in me a fury that was hard to staunch. What use to anyone a laced handkerchief redolent with the scent of memory or a tarnished silver frame where looking out, her sad sepia smile was worthless to all but me. And then the irony of a thousand bank notes undiscovered beneath the browned wallpaper lining of an empty drawer. I have not touched them since.

It was the end of a laborious and hot week, not that I would have complained much about that for since she died the work had become a welcome diversion from the alternative which was nothing at all. I was never much one for sympathising with a neighbour's grief but loneliness swallowed me with its indifference just like anybody else.

My solace, I suppose, was my wife's presence in the few material possessions she left behind; a shrine, if you like, where I could still stroke her face or touch her hand again even when she was no longer there. And then, like some acid tongue that licks its destruction into metal, they stripped me of it all.

Timing. Timing was the thing. A few minutes might have made the difference at the end of the day, but a woman had spluttered into the forecourt, speech bubbles of steam hissing up from under the bonnet of the Land Rover and those minutes had vanished. By the time I drove to the house no more than a mile away, they had already stolen my wife from me. The back door drooped from one remaining hinge as though suffering from a bad Saturday night's kicking, the bruised imprint of a boot smudged beneath the bent handle. Inside I could track easily the path of the intruders, first through the small kitchen where heavy soles had dinted the lino and then on to the parlour which had transformed from a tidy sanctuary into a place of chaos. The smell of their breaths remained in the stilled air chewing its way into memory like a slap. On again through to the bedroom (for ours was just a bungalow of modest size) and to where the breaking of my heart became complete.

The only item to remain outwardly untouched was our bed, but I got rid of that anyway once the police had finished with the fingerprinting next day; everything else had been either taken or smashed and thrown aside. In the corner her dressing table hunched over unnaturally on its stubby legs, posture spoiled by the amputation of a side-mirror which once reflected her lovely profile. Gone was the string of pearls that always seemed to dangle impatiently until the night of some infrequent 'do'. Gone also were her Bible and wedding ring and, of course, her presence. Whatever else they took it was this last that violated me the most.

I took to walking my way to and from work after that for it was somehow the only source of comfort I could find. At the garage time became unimportant with the monotony of engines to tune and petrol tanks to fill but in the surrounding countryside hedgerows sustained their growth and continued to flourish into late summer. The perfume of honeysuckle in particular accompanied my walks each time and I would often pick a token bunch just to keep the kitchen table from its bareness. Then one day as I stretched for a stem I noticed something snagged in the undergrowth and tugged it free.

Her handkerchief.

55

At first it was not recognisable as such but as I teased the material from my palm the intricate laced border emerged grubbily and the embroidered initial of her name showed from a corner. 'E', Elizabeth. I pressed it hard into my face hoping for some vestige of scent but there was none, only the dispassionate odour of earth and air. Yet what elation to be connected once more and feel the touch of her fingers through the fabric and have her belong to me again.

It was only later that I thought it strange to have uncovered one of her belongings in such an obscure place. So I returned to the same spot and searched again but the blackthorn was densely packed and its thorns tore bloody ribbons across the backs of my hands. I unearthed nothing more in the end and returned to the house empty-handed yet the incident had aroused in me a spark of hope that if one of her belongings had been discarded as the thieves made their flight then perhaps there might be more. I could only think that they might have been thrown from a car window as worthless spoils. And so my search, in earnest, began.

The police had been less than enthusiastic following up the burglary and got nowhere with the fingerprints. The 'usual opportunists,' they said. 'Impossible to pursue the case without enough evidence,'' they said. 'Sorry.' It was something I had to accept. Something I could do little about.

I learned to hate those bastards too. But if I couldn't nail the culprits myself then at least I could try to appease my growing anger by continuing the hunt for her lost things and this I did on every journey to work for weeks. Scrutinising the hedges as carefully as any sniper examining an impending target I explored my way along every foot of undergrowth between home and garage. It must, in truth, have looked an odd sort of sight; my recently-turned white hair as shocking as summer snow among the brambles and the silvered blade of a scythe glinting erratically in amongst the blackthorn. More than once a neighbour stopped to inquire about my well-being and bade me the time of day but really to confirm to themselves my increasing eccentricity since the event.

On the third morning though, I came upon my second find. It had descended deep into the ditch below and was almost swallowed by thick mulch preventing me from seeing it at first. It was her family bible and as its flaccid cover moulded damply into the contours of my hand I thought of the last time it had been used - to write her own name beneath the list of kin already scribed inside the back page. Later that day I set the Bible near the stove to dry out knowing that its contents would never properly recover from their weathering but equally knowing that, for me, the words of the gospels had now become inconsequential.

Over the following weeks my explorations became as enlightening as they were frantic and it seemed like the very soul of humanity was unwittingly being exposed. Of the three rotting animal carcasses I uncovered, one was still recognisable as my own cat, gone missing not long since with no explanation, but probably run over and dumped without ceremony. There were disgusting things too, things that I do not much care to consign to memory but these were negated somewhat by unexpected delights, amongst them the fragile beauty of an empty wren's nest still sweet and perfect in its tininess; an old thrupenny bit greened by history and the elements and cock pheasant feathers evacuated from unsuspecting tails. These and more were the secreted treasures surprising me during my daily hunts and it made the disappointments of discovering nothing more of hers more bearable.

In the house I did my best to repair the damaged dressing table and returned her Bible and handkerchief to their rightful places, displaying my other discovered treasures alongside. Together they became a story onto themselves and I began to believe that some good could actually come of something bad.

After a life as a man of few words I found myself sitting before the mirrored shrine in the evenings, conversing with my wife in a way that I had neglected to do while she was alive. Gradually then, in a quiet and almost unnoticeable way, my life began to heal and unlike other folk who complained of the downward turn on their businesses, work at the garage had actually picked up. My days became measured by the journeys of discovery each morning followed by the satisfying application of my labour during the day.

Meanwhile, emerging through the soft greens of summer was a promise of autumn that carried with it the beginnings of a barer landscape, but by then I had completed my search of the hedges between home and garage. The rage that had at one time been all-consuming had gradually dissipated and life seemed, if not meaningful, then at least more optimistic. In short, I found solace in the unexpected and freely resigned myself to it.

Time in the workplace was swallowed by MOT checks, engine services and an infinite amount of blow-in custom throughout the day and when one morning the young son of a neighbour unexpectedly arrived to drop his car off with a clutch problem I was happy to give it some attention before his promised return. The vehicle's bodywork itself was not in the best of shape and the engine had been souped up enough for me to know that it had its purposes and was probably being used accordingly. At this I found myself smiling with the thought of my own youth, my first car and that same irresponsible passion for risk and danger, so I knew any repairs I did would not last for very long.

That the clutch was the problem was obvious, but as business was slower than usual that particular day I gave the car more consideration than it probably deserved. I do not know why I opened the boot. There was no need to. Everything that called for my attention was accessible from the outside and there was little reason to seek a jack or anything else that the boot might have contained. It released reluctantly, the hook snagging momentarily before springing wide like the mouth of some great white shark. A spare tyre nestled in its proper position alongside the jack which was secured by two screws one of which seemed to have made its way loose. As purchase to make it tight I grabbed the grubby scrap of cloth lying near my hand and once the job was done went to set it back from where it had come. But as the rag left my grip and the familiar fabric unfurled into the delicate fingers of a woman's evening glove I knew that one more spoil was to be added now to the collection and that later it too would be returned to its rightful home.

He was pleasant on his return. A pretty blond girl dropped him off and I heard her say she'd probably see him later on. We discussed the problem of the clutch and even had a bit of a laugh about the ineptitude of the police and how they couldn't control the boy racers and joy riders doing handbrake turns down on the dual carriageway most evenings. He joked that you could get away with murder these days given that the courts were overloaded with cases they couldn't keep up with. His tyres spun as he drove away, the skunk-like stench of burning rubber left to linger on the garage forecourt and exhaust fumes forming a kind of question mark in the space that had been vacated.

I locked the place up as soon as I could and hummed cheerfully to myself on the way back home, for after all there was something to be said for a good day's work. It did cross my mind that I was never going to find the matching glove now or anything else of hers for that matter but those thoughts hardly mattered anymore. There was no telling when the brake cable would snap, probably not until the car was under pressure, and by then it would already be too late.

If I had a mind to, I'd listen to the local late-night news after I'd brushed my teeth.

For Those Who Wait

ACROSS THE RIVER BLINDED WINDOWS STARED their dull indifference over the water. The old asylum, derelict now, of course, its facade of red brick faded to the colour of spent leaves. In the past she had scanned the river from a ribboned sky-light in the roof, every day seeking out the herons who faithfully returned each year, their nests shocking like bizarre haircuts among the shallows; this, always, her fragile connection to the world outside. Now the pulse of the river's ebb and flow acknowledged her return as its wetness seeped through the soles of her shoes and the urgency of its current urged her on towards her former home.

In the early morning all was quiet along the towpath and no one disturbed her short walk from the bus stop to the bridge. Somewhere distant towards the innards of the town a car horn sounded but the only other noise she could hear was a sad whispering from hospital bricks. She stepped across the wooden slats of the bridge to the other side, careful suddenly of her footing, for her legs had never really become accustomed to walking more length than that of a grey corridor.

The track leading to the building was steeper than she remembered and loose shale threatened to stab her ankles which showed white in the gap between trousers and shoes. Eventually she reached an entrance where interlopers had discarded their human detritus onto the gravel. An empty aerosol can, its nozzle oozing like a bad nose bleed, lay where it was flung and the tip of a syringe needle spiked up from the ground as though groping for its next hit. Planks of wood designed to prevent entry to the building had long ago been vandalised offering easy access to anyone who might risk crossing the threshold.

Turning, she glanced back in the direction from which she had come, taking in the steep bank to the river; a river where once she had witnessed a woman, younger even than herself, drown inside a hug of swirling water.

She shuttered her eyes for a second but carried on inside the building's shell where the atmosphere, although horribly sinister and oppressive, did not intimidate her. Every passageway's turn, every unevenness of flooring were as familiar to her as if they were a map tattooed upon her skin. Gaps in the boarded windows allowed only enough light to see where the taggers had been busy killing the already dying walls with their graffiti. Underneath a light switch someone had randomly scrawled a name, Richard, and above, still in bold, even letters, a sign read 'Clinic of the Insane'.

She carried on into the growing gloom of rooms where no brightness had dared to challenge even during times when the curtainless windows had been intact, until she met the beginnings of a central staircase. From there she would be able to follow a path to the landing above, and above that, and then above that again, until she arrived at the attic rooms. But she knew that her legs, even now throbbing like some ancient and failing contraption, would never see her reach beyond the first floor.

Standing alone in the vast reception space that would have been her first encounter there as a teenage girl, she listened to the continuing soft murmur of the bricks. And then ahead, a different yet familiar sort of sound: a rasping, like the breath of some garrotted and dying animal, and she was suddenly vigilant. In small steps she made her way forward, her hands unexpectedly reaching for the flaked walls as she inadvertently dislodged a broken relic of Saint Teresa whose smile, even now, held its cruel capacity to mock. The rasping up ahead had stopped but its following silence brought with it something else; an emotion that she had thought had been buried and finally put to rest - longing.

His old office was not difficult to find for its location remained at the bottom of the west wing corridor where windows had once looked out, not upon the river, but on the town. The grated breathing had started up again followed by a silence, the rhythm of both like a song to her now with every beat matching her closing footfall. Him.

He was seated, straight-backed on a lonely chair in the middle of the room as if he had been expecting her for a long time. His eyes were hard to make out but she knew that they would never have lost their blue, almost purple edging, and inward towards the pupil, those sparks of yellow among the darkness of the iris.

Details.

Details would always be her accomplice. Mostly about him. And others. But also about herself. They were the spaces between words in a sentence, the specks of dust drifting in stagnant air, the taste of her lip on her tongue before she fell asleep.

"Cora."

It was that same rough breathlessness of her name he had used when they met there and had evidently never lost. Speech was suddenly alien in her mouth and her body would permit only a curt movement of the head in affirmation. For a moment in the gathered dimness of the decaying office their familiarity felt like a kiss, a parted mouth stroking the paleness of her throat, a swift lick of tongue across her now creeping neck. She barely believed that he could still have that hold upon her.

"Here," he was saying as his chair scraped from beneath him, "Take this. Sit."

She did as she was told and waited as he searched for something else, and finding an old stool slid it across the floor in front of her with his foot. He sat down with care, the lowness of the stool making a contortion of his legs and forcing his eyes to look upwards into hers. He will not be comfortable with that, she thought, and allowed herself a small smile. From outside, seeping through the window boards, came the sound of children's voices probably making their way to school, the harsh obscenities spattered amongst their speech the only discernible words. Cora was dismayed by it, the fact that the worst culprit was undeniably female and worse, young. But as the voices passed and left behind their residue of distaste she finally spoke.

"You seemed to be expecting me."

He hesitated before answering, another practice he had seemingly retained.

"I have been expecting you back forever."

"And how long is that?"

"About a week."

It was impossible not to, so she laughed.

"You can still make a girl smile," she said.

"I thought you might have been intrigued and come because of the anniversary," he said, choosing to ignore the irony of her remark although she knew that he had noted it. Nothing ever had or would ever go unnoticed. "And besides," he continued, "I know you miss me." His sudden use of the present tense was deliberate and this time it was she who chose to do the ignoring, but he took her silence as acknowledgement and continued. "A decade since they boarded the place up and they couldn't even demolish it. Instead they marked their dirty past with that brand new hospital next door. They invited me back as a dignitary for the opening ceremony."

"They?"

"They."

She wouldn't get any more out of him than that.

"So," he went on, "after all that farce I thought about coming here just in case you'd show up. I'm leaving tonight and this was my last gamble."

The exchange between them had taken no longer than a few minutes but now that she was seated and calm Cora had been able to survey him better as he talked.

He had aged well. She could see that. There had been no thinning of the hair that accompanied the maturing of most men, no greying either although it was a harder condition to detect when he had always had hair the colour of raw thatch. Only his hands showed much signs of change, hands that once owned the softness of a man unaccustomed to physical labour and could express a complex emotion in a single movement were now pleached tightly together on his lap. The knuckles peaked as white as small icebergs between his fingers as he squeezed and released them subconsciously.

"You actually thought I'd willingly come back to this?" She made a sweeping motion with her arms. "Really?"

"You did though, didn't you, Cora. So why?"

Her reply had for a long time grown like a seed inside her head. How her voice would be strong. How that half of her that did not long for him would show the raw hatred behind her eyes. But instead the words came out of her mouth as weakly as the trickle from a dripping tap.

"I came back to find what was taken from me. My soul. My soul and also my child whose life you stole from me."

"The world was different then. Surely you know that."

It was said with such little feeling that Cora could almost laugh again, but this time at herself for being naïve enough to believe he might have changed.

"I know that we no longer live in a world where vulnerable people are incarcerated for nothing, if that's what you mean?"

"Nothing? You were hardly incarcerated for nothing."

She could detect the hardness skulking around the edges of his voice, the disillusionment still encased within the warped shell of his psyche.

"And remember that I protected and looked after you," he continued, "when I didn't have to. For all those years."

"Twenty years was a long time to be beholden to someone," she said, the sarcasm stinging like raw bile at the back of her throat. "Are you saying that I owe you a debt of gratitude?"

Now that her eyes had become fully accustomed to the darkness she could see better any inflections in his facial expression. The mouth, so much like her own with its reluctant and involuntary smile, the small white teeth, partially showing between his parted lips, the careless indifference flaunted in the hollow of his sucked in cheeks. His shoulders rose briefly in a shrug.

"If the cap fits," he said. He rose from the discomfort of the stool and stood before her, reaching out a hand as though to touch her cheek.

"Where is she?"

Cora's own voice sounded foreign to her now, but this was the reason she had come after all and it needed to be finished.

"Our daughter, you mean? They buried her in a grave out there somewhere." At this he signalled towards the window. "It was unmarked. You'll not find it."

She got up, standing almost eye to eye with him, the brother who had shaped her sin of pregnancy into his own deceit. An aspiring young doctor destined for greatness, he had been the germ of her abandonment when their family's shame ensured that no one else would claim her as their own. Those years of interminable hardship had endured from the moment of her eventual release, leeching from her bones both day and night. But she had been patient. She had known, of course, of his visit there for she had seen his name emblazoned across the front of all the papers, 'Eminent psychiatrist returns for opening of new hospital.'

He had been right about their daughter's remains, but that would not prevent her even now from salvaging both their souls. She waited for the familiar flicker of his eyelids as he bent to kiss her mouth, a momentary lack of concentration that would always prove to be his undoing, and slid the blade easily into the beauty of his throat. For in the end it would always come down to this.

And, of course, the details.

Do Not Disturb

THE GIRL BEHIND THE RECEPTION COUNTER had, pinned to her blouse, a type of living badge. It moved with the rise and fall of her breasts and read simply Jess followed by the title of 'Assistant Manager' and the logo of the hotel.

Richard had been observing her for several moments, gauging her reaction to the ignoramus standing ahead of him and admiring her diplomacy as she fended off the man's evident self-importance. The foyer was empty of people apart from the three of them and the exchange between girl and guest rang easily off the putty-painted walls. It filled the space with an ugliness that clung to the furniture's upholstery like aged sewage. Richard abhorred needless rudeness, especially when it was directed at the undeserving, and he shifted from one tired foot to the other in frustrated irritation.

"I do apologise, sir," the girl was saying. "There seems to have been some kind of misunderstanding about your room, 215. I'll see to it personally that you're moved to something more appropriate for the rest of your stay."

Her fingertips began tapping at a keyboard concealed under the counter but her eyes continued to roam the man's face and the upward curl of her mouth remained pleasantly static. The living badge on her chest however became perfectly still.

Breathe. It seemed to be saying. *Breathe.*

"I hope it's got a fucking decent bed this time. Does the retard who took my booking not know the difference between two singles and a double?"

Fragments of a recent meal peppered themselves on the girl, Jess's, sleeve. Without looking she flicked them off with the back of her hand and carried on typing. A gigantic clock ticked its minutes across the room. The fax machine hummed its way back into life. And when the tapping of the keyboard ceased the smile was still on the assistant manager's face. Then she reached behind her to where an assortment of keys hung like fruit bats from the wall and pulled one out.

"Here you are, Mr Goodfellow," she said. "This room has got the best fucking bed in the whole hotel."

The badge began to live again. Up and down. Up and down.

Mr Goodfellow stared at the key lying between them on the counter as though it had arrived there by alien intervention.

"Get me the fucking manager," he spat, his clenched knuckles throbbing like small mountains on the back of his hands.

"The manager isn't here, sir. I'm afraid you'll have to deal with his assistant instead."

She lifted the key, dangling it in the space between his eyes and inside their scrunched up resentment she was satisfied to see that they had the same nondescript hue of water in a fish tank. She recognised then that he would not have the courage to confront her further.

Silently shrugging her own contempt towards him she felt the key leave her fingers and with a mumbled threat of getting her sacked the man skulked off towards the lift as she knew he would.

"Room 303," she shouted into his back. "Enjoy the rest of your stay, sir."

Richard's feet settled in the indentations his predecessor had made on the carpet. He straightened up his tie, secured the button of his suit jacket and waited for Jess to turn her attention to him. In profile she was even prettier than full face and her eyes held the lift's doors until they sucked themselves together. Only then did she turn her attention back to him. "I'm very sorry," she said, her vocal chords struggling to gravel out the words. "My mother would be ashamed of me using terrible language like that but sometimes it's the only way to deal with people like him."

Richard wondered how she might have known that he was not, himself, one of those people but refrained from comment. Instead he stood silently waiting for her to carry on speaking and in the meantime studied her features more closely. He had, after all, spent most of his adult life doing just that with complete strangers; a job he had come to loathe but could never seem to escape from. He was used to weighing up personality types by how people dressed, the way they moved, even the angle they held their heads when they spoke, but this girl, this young woman Jess, she would take more than the normal two minutes to figure out if he had the inclination.

"Excuse me sir, but do you have a reservation?" Her voice was back to normal, her smile more genuine and relaxed than it had been.

"I'm afraid I don't," explained Richard," but if you wouldn't mind, I'd like the room he didn't want." His eyes flicked towards the closed doors of the lift whose numbers were flashing their way upward through the hotel floors.

If Jess was surprised by the request it didn't show. Instead she leaned across the counter and whispered, "He was absolutely right, you know. Apart from the beds the room was dark and not very nice. It faces straight out onto the rubbish skips at the side. Are you sure you want to take it? I can offer you something nicer. More light."

"No really, that's fine. I'll pay in advance if that's okay. I have the cash."

He felt in an inside pocket for his wallet and tugged it out. Jess had started typing again but paused to ask him how long his stay might be.

"Just the one night," Richard replied pushing two fifty pound notes over the counter and replacing his wallet. "Is that going to be enough?"

"Of course Mr ...?"

"Hamilton. Richard Hamilton."

"Of course, Mr Hamilton, and that will cover dinner as well

although you'll have to hurry as chef is on last orders in the restaurant right now."

Richard told her that he'd go straight through and come back for his bag later if that was okay with her and she smiled when she said it was. He was glad that her teeth weren't perfect and that one eye-tooth stuck out slightly from the rest for, if anything, it made her open face all the more attractive.

He took the key she was offering and left her to deal with some further arrivals while he went in search of food and found that despite the lateness of the hour the restaurant was still reasonably full. There was a table for two recently vacated in a pleasant position beside the window and Richard was happy to wait while the waitress prepared it with an individual setting.

Already he knew the meal he would order; fillet steak, blue, which he would trust the chef to get right and with it a plain salad with vinaigrette on the side.

He inspected the wine list for a nice smooth South African Cabernet Sauvignon, more expensive than he'd have liked but one of his few indulgences when he sometimes dined alone and he ordered a bottle knowing that half of it would be wasted.

When it came, Richard ate the food slowly concentrating on the soft texture of the meat and its flavour in his mouth. The wine was not exactly to his taste but it was close enough not to comment on should he have thought of writing a review later on the internet. He passed on dessert and instead satisfied his need for something sweet with a highly sugared cappuccino accompanied by a chocolate mint. Only when he finished did he realise the room was empty of diners and the waitress had begun laying tables for tomorrow's breakfast. She had been attentive and competent at her job, deserving the generous ten pound tip Richard slid underneath his coffee cup as he got up.

Jess was still behind reception when he went back to collect his bag and although her demeanour was composed and friendly he wondered what she did to relax after her shift. At least being self-employed meant that he himself could pick and choose his clients at will, but having to compulsorily deal with the public was an entirely different matter as his wife Marie would contest to. In her many years working behind the desk at the local police station the abuse she'd endured had been terrible. She'd been puked on, called vile names, threatened by junkies, petty criminals and worse but she had never brought the emotional consequences home with her except to tell him verbatim, the facts. Her uncomplicated honesty had always been the thing he loved most about her; her honesty and her faithfulness.

They had met ten years earlier when he was asked to assess the psychological condition of a young teenager recently taken into custody for anti-social behaviour. Marie had been on duty at the time, dealing with the usual flak of her working day, but she had stayed behind to help Richard with the long process of form-filling afterwards. He knew immediately that she loved him, not out of arrogance on his part, but simply that she could never manage to hide it very well. He in turn, loved everything about her, but in the knowledge that that was not quite the same as actually loving the person that she was. The awareness that she never seemed to notice, while he struggled with it every single day, was increasingly difficult to bear. That and his own duplicity.

The hotel room was, as Jess had admitted, dingy and uninviting. But it was at the end of a corridor and therefore quiet which Richard had expected. Out of habit he removed his shoes, placing them neatly on the floor of the wardrobe and turned on the trouser press. Street light was wrestling its way through the smudged glass of the window and as he looked out Richard could decipher below, several multi-coloured bins and a couple of skips. There was a certain kind of beauty in the way someone had taken time to line them up; the skips looked like gargantuan bookends with the bins in between as though they were as important as a row of plant pots in someone's immaculate garden. And for the first time in a while Richard felt himself smile.

He draped his jacket over the back of a chair and slipped off his trousers, carefully sliding them into the press. A green light continued to glow and when it turned to red Richard knew that the creases would be as sharp as an origami pleat of paper. He perched himself on one of the beds to wait, feeling the dangle of his legs, remembering suddenly a time in his childhood when, with his father, they had sat together on a riverbank dipping their toes into cold, black water. All of his memories seemed to be thus: full of simplicity and warmth which Richard supposed was the precedent for his chosen career. His ability to assess the character of complete strangers demanded patience and empathy in equal measures, both of which he had inherited from his father. How ironic it seemed to him then that he had always been able to fool the world into thinking he was someone he was not.

As the minutes ticked on silently in the clockless room Richard relaxed back onto the bed and allowed his eyes to close. The headboard rested against the thin partition wall dividing him from the room next door and a muffled hum of a television set seeped its way through with the ease of a ghost gliding through a slab of concrete. Richard prayed that that would be all he would hear and for the guests in there to spare him the stifled inhibitions of the lust which often accompanied him on his lonely hotel stays. Without bothering to sit up he reached for the hotel phone that sat on the table between the beds and dialled reception.

"Yes. Can I help you?" The female voice was new and Richard was glad that the other girl had possibly been relieved of her shift.

"Could you put me through to Room 303 please?"

"Of course, sir. Just a second."

The line silenced itself for a moment and Richard's heartbeat pumped loudly in his free ear.

Then the connection. A man's voice. Gruff.

"Yes. 303."

"Is that Keith?" Richard was now sitting upright on the bed, his socked bare legs making him feel ridiculous and uncharacteristically vulnerable. The sweat at his temples leaked and started trickling towards his chin.

"Richard, yeah?" said the voice.

"That's right. I contacted you yesterday."

"Jesus, I was wondering where the hell you were. Sorry about the cock-up. They gave me a duff room but you've obviously been set straight at reception. Anyway, come on up to 303. Everything's ready to go and I'll see to it we won't be disturbed."

Richard remembered the receptionist's badge from earlier on and how it had seemed to freeze as she decided what to say next.

"I've changed my mind," he said. Silence entombed the line between the two phones like a death. "I've changed my mind," Richard repeated stupidly trying to prepare himself for what he knew must come. Keith's intake of air was a rifle shot before implosion.

"What the fuck, you homo creep. You've kept me waiting half the night like the virgin queer you are, just to leave me hanging on waiting here. Well, it's your loss, you wanker, but I'm still going to fucking bill you for wasting my time. And while I'm at it maybe give your wife a ring to tell her the good news that her husband..."

Richard rested the phone back into its cradle and released his hand as if it had been in contact with something contaminated. He peeled himself up from the bed and walked to the bathroom where the toiletries he had brought with him were sitting beside the sink. The shaving gel felt warm on his skin and the razor slid smoothly along his cheeks and chin like melted butter on warm bread. In the mirror some other Richard watched his movements with a mixture of indifference and pride, each slow meticulous flow of the blade something to despise and savour all at once. When it was done and he was satisfied that his ablutions were completed to his usual high standards Richard moved back to the bedroom and released his trousers from the press. The static on the material tingled against the skin of his legs as he pulled them on but the creases were acceptably sharp and precise and appropriate.

He didn't know when but Richard realised suddenly that he had started to hum, the sound buzzing between his lips in sharp little bursts of melody that he could not quite identify but liked nonetheless. He hummed as he picked up his jacket from the chair to put it on and hummed too as he neatly tied the laces of his shoes in a double bow. And he hummed as he searched for the hotel writing paper inside the desk drawer. Only when he sat down to write did Richard allow himself the silence of thought.

The whole situation was ludicrous, unplanned until two days ago when he had finally decided to find the man he was and end the lie he had always seemed to half-live. The pen moved between his fingers forming words that would explain all and nothing at all.

Making sure that he tucked away the chair and smoothed down the bedcover Richard walked the few feet to the bathroom door. He was glad it wouldn't be Jess, the assistant manager, as he'd liked her and it would probably change her life – change anybody's life. The words on the piece of A4 paper appeared small and insignificant but at least he had written them with care in his beautiful copperplate script:

'Anyone can stop a man's life, but no one his death; a thousand doors open on to it.'

Then with one hand he pressed the paper against one of the door panels and with the other produced from his pocket a small globule of blu-tac that he always carried for emergencies at work. For it was not in Richard's nature to purposely destroy things and he did not wish to damage the door, but at least when they eventually pulled it off, his sign would not have left any mark.

Two Voices

IF YOU LISTEN CAREFULLY YOU WILL hear it, the beating of my heart as its lifeblood gushes and slops against my ribs. Gradually it moves, thumping and pumping along the endless tubes and caverns of its journey, to the centre of my mind. Thump, thump. Slop, slop. Today and yesterday. Tomorrow and forever. Fear.

It is morning and I allow my eyes to lie lazily shut and think of Jamie. He is the voice inside keeping me sane, keeping me from the hopelessness that threatens to engulf me, keeping me alive.

I listen to the soft movements from the kitchen below where my mother prepares breakfast. Ours is a small house and every movement reverberates through its frame which means that when I cry I must be careful to pull the duvet tightly around my head. I am thirteen and crying, I have learned, is only for wimps and nerds. Jamie never cries.

Muffled voices seep through the floorboards and a door closes downstairs. My father has gone to work. He used to come and kiss me goodbye, but once when he saw me scrunched within the duvet, he closed the door and never came again. This I understood and it never diminished my love for him. My mother calls, "James, get up or you'll be late," and I bury myself deeper beneath the covers listening to Jamie saying, "Come on, James. Get moving – you've a bus to catch," and because I know I have to, I comply.

It is October and autumn leaves crackle beneath the soles of my shiny black brogues. I walk to catch the bus, up Chester Avenue and past the crumbling gateposts of the municipal park. I am in no hurry but Jamie is vying for attention in my head, encouraging me to speed up. Then I see them standing in silhouette, lounging carelessly against the wooden bus shelter as smoke from their cigarettes drift slowly outwards in staccatoed pockets of puff. The one who is closest turns her eyes on me.

And so it begins.

Jamie hisses the words I have heard in my head every day for nearly a year. "You can do it today. Do it today." But I am James and know that today will be the same as any other.

Four pairs of eyes are on me now and like heat seeking missiles they hone in on their target with perfect precision. Backs straighten and cigarette butts are obliterated beneath designer heels.

The attack begins.

"We like your shiny shoes, James," purrs the first, malice sticking like cream to her glossy lips. "Mummy clean them for you, did she?" and the others close in, smelling the scent of the kill and waiting excitedly for this morning's share of the spoils.

I feel the moisture on my back as sweat sucks at my clean shirt. But today I am saved by the bus as screeching brakes herald a sudden scramble for the doors. The survival of the fittest. Strong to the back seats, the weak, standing room only at the front.

It takes twenty-two minutes to get to school. I have timed it on my ultra sophisticated diver's watch my parents bought me for my birthday. It is hidden beneath the chewed cuffs of my jumper and I feel its pulse travelling up my arm, one second for two heartbeats marking the growing apprehension churning in the pit of my stomach.

"Deep breaths," Jamie says. "We're nearly there."

But I cannot control my rising panic and feel the sour taste of sick rising up in the back of my throat. Up ahead I see the school gates and hold my breath in an effort to prevent myself from throwing up. My lungs are burning but I manage to hold on until the bus pulls up and we pour out onto the gum-peppered pavement. A large glob of spit hits me on the back of the neck, seeping down the collar of my shirt and resting at the top of my spine. Jamie does not miss his chance, "Get the bastard's name, James. Glob the bastard back." But I can only feel the slow drag of my feet carrying me through the gates and into hell.

The locker area buzzes. Forgotten rugby kits spill from holdalls in sweaty bundles and are kicked contemptuously across the floor. A girl from my year walks by and unexpectedly stops to ask, "Can I check with your maths homework, James?" Her name is Hazel. She has the skinniest pair of legs I have ever seen, but she is nice. "Later," I say and she continues down the corridor, her skirt swaying effortlessly as she walks.

"Oooh, James has got himself a girlfriend then. Tasty bit of stuff, is she?"

It is Billy Greg, king spitter. We stand eyeball to eyeball, our lips practically touching.

"Tell him to piss off, James," urges Jamie from somewhere faraway in my head. I want to. In fact, I want to hit Billy Greg so hard that I smash his beautiful straight teeth right to the back of his throat. But I can't, and I won't, and I know I never will.

"She's not my girlfriend," I tell him, reaching to close the locker door and make my escape. It is a mistake. Billy glimpses the watch and grabs my wrist like a vice. His fingers are unbelievably soft and I sense Jamie sniggering at this unexpected femininity.

"And what's this, James?" Billy snarls. "A nice new watch from Mummy and Daddy. You kept that one a bit quiet."

I am getting scared now, the smell of the locker room is overpowering, the tension unbearable. Some of the boys have gone to class but none of those who have stayed will champion me. I am on my own with a stupid voice in my head and a useless body to go with it.

The vice–like grip tightens.

"Give me the watch, nerd," Billy whispers, his breath hot in my ear, but I do not want to relinquish the watch. It is the only possession I have managed to keep secret and I do not know how to explain its disappearance to my parents.

Jamie screams at me, "James. Punch his lights out. Keep the watch. It's ours." And for a fleeting moment I almost feel like I could do it. But the bell rings and the moment is gone, my bravery banished by the reality of an ever-present threat even Jamie cannot erase. I remove the precious present from my wrist and place it into the hand of my tormentor.

"Coward," accuses Jamie. He will not speak to me until later when his disgust at my weakness diminishes.

Billy saunters away and the others, disappointed that there has been no bloodletting, make their way to class. My eyes remain dry. There are no tears left for me to cry. I am thirteen years old and I wonder what it was, the terrible thing I did in some past life, to pay such penance now.

My parents tried to help but their intervention only made things worse and in the end I pretended the bullying had stopped. The only one I share it with now is Jamie but today his silence makes my isolation more intolerable and even Hazel has forgotten her earlier request to cross check our homework. It was such a little thing but I feel the hurt of her forgetfulness acutely and the fear in me melts into a kind of resigned despair.

Today the journey home allows some respite. The big, tough, macho boys remain in school with the big, tough, macho rugby playing teachers. The girls don their makeup and gossip together on street corners. Nobody is interested in James Baker anymore.

Our house is empty. My mother has left the key beneath a flowerpot and I let myself in. The house smells nice. Everything is tidy. Outside I hear the familiar noise of the traffic trundling down our road.

Jamie begins to forgive me and starts up a conversation in my head, "Tell them you lost it at PE, James. Get it back tomorrow." But his voice is coming from a distant place and I am not listening. I go to the closet beneath the stairs. My dad's box of tools is there and I rummage to find the old rope he saves 'just in case'. I wonder if it is long enough. Thump, thump. Slop, slop. Strange that the fear is still here when I feel nothing but absolute calm. Strange, too, that for the first time Jamie has begun to panic.

"Don't James. Don't let them win," he screams, but I tie an end of the rope to the banister and tug it tightly, feeling my weight on it and testing its strength. I make a kind of noose with the other end and place it over my head. Will it hurt? Will it be immediate?

You know what? It really doesn't matter.

The Babies

MATILDA DARLING WAS LATE. THE BEADS of sweat that bulged like miniature bubble wrap across her brow had caused her normally manageable chestnut curls to lie slicked in tiny question marks on her forehead. But at least the library hadn't closed. According to the clock she had just twelve minutes to exchange her mother's books and return the unwatched DVD she had borrowed the previous week. Time enough, Matilda thought, the cold metal of the turnstile briefly resistant against her thighs; time enough in view of the exertions she had put herself through just to get there.

She considered the circumstances that had delayed her and sighed. Why parents couldn't collect their children on time from school was a question she had struggled with for a while and then for them to turn up late without explanation or apology, well that was simply the worst kind of example for their offspring.

Yet over the years Matilda had learned that for her pupils' sakes, it was better to hand them over without comment and seethe inwardly about it later on when she could allow herself to rage into the coldness of her double duvet and wonder why people who didn't even like them, would consider having children at all. But now because she'd missed her lift, she had to hot foot it to the local bus stop and finally race through the town centre like a banshee to make it before closing time, resembling something out of a Harry Potter novel.

The thought, however, did not altogether disagree with her and she smiled.

At the counter, Matilda handed the books and DVD over to a man whose washed-out eyes matched the grey drabness of his cardigan and whose unclipped fingernails tapped irritatingly on the keyboard as he typed in her name. She steeled herself for what would inevitably come next.

"Thank you, darling," he said, chuckling as though it was the first time the joke had ever been made. "Anything else, darling?"

Matilda chewed hard on the terrible word that always lingered somewhere near the back of her tongue on such occasions. One day she would lose the will to check its progress into open air, either that or change her name by deed poll, but somehow such an undertaking demanded more resolve than she could ever manage to muster up. Instead she turned away without comment and headed back towards the exit, stopping only when she reached the glazed waiting area near the door.

It was her favourite place in the building and Matilda would have visited the library every day just to enjoy the view out onto the bay, as long as the tide was in. Today, though, the water had receded enough to reveal, on the mudflats left behind, the coughed-up debris of people's lives. Discarded bedsteads and abandoned trolleys copulated together in the sludgy brownness and tomorrow, if she came, Matilda knew there would be something different to observe. The scene was something that was both fascinating and grotesque and left her feeling more voyeuristic than she would have liked but it was hard to pull her eyes away.

Until she noticed the pram.

It was parked awkwardly in the corner as though, having not quite managed to get the angle correct, the owner had simply abandoned it where it was and Matilda was intrigued.

The pram reminded her of a miniature hearse, the big black body oddly old-fashioned on its chromed wheels whose spokes were now glinting like sharpened penknives in the late afternoon sunshine. Only in magazines where the well-to-do advertised for traditional nanny services, had Matilda seen an example of such a magnificent perambulator before. Certainly anyone she knew who had a baby (which was the multitude of single mothers at her school), used those lightweight buggy things that concertinaed like an accordion when not required. She had observed one young mum on the bus deftly performing just such a task that afternoon.

The pram did not obstruct Matilda's path to the exit but nevertheless she was drawn like a thieving magpie to view its contents and found herself looking down upon two of the most beautiful babies she had ever set eyes on. Neither was awake although it was hard to see how the smaller of the two could sleep comfortably considering the disproportionate size of the other. Yet in some strange way and despite their obvious differences, the babies seemed to compliment each other and something inside Matilda stirred with a longing she normally preferred to keep at bay. She peered down into the pram and examined more closely the two miracles of nature that she could, if she so wished, now reach out and touch.

The larger of the two lay on its back, plump arms resting peacefully on a delicate filigreed shawl. Matilda could only marvel at the baby's dimpled cheeks and prettily curled eyelashes looking as though they might unfold in wakefulness at any moment. Its bed-partner rested on its side, tufts of hair the colour of corn shocking their way in small eruptions from the surface of a pale scalp. Matilda inspected the mottled skin, so transparent that it reminded her quite alarmingly of a naked chicken freshly hatched from the egg; the result surely of some imbalance in growth between the twins. That is, assuming that that was what they were.

She started to bend closer towards them, her need to feel their baby breaths outweighing for once her sense of propriety, when a hand caught her shoulder and somewhere close a voice was saying, "Can I help you with something?"

Matilda straightened, embarrassed at being caught in some innocent act that she knew could be construed otherwise and turned to face the person she assumed to be the babies' mother.

"Oh," she said, her face reddening with alarming speed. "I'm just admiring your children. They're very beautiful."

The woman standing before her smiled sweetly. It was a

smile Matilda sensed had been delivered to others before and would be produced again many times more. Yet the cobalt eyes that fixed her in their gaze remained strangely chilled as though winter and summer had simultaneously visited a face where they could not easily be released. For a moment the two women looked at each other. Matilda's mouth opened and closed silently like a fish nibbling on a hook until the baited words arrived to reel her in.

"They're not real babies," said the woman, her own mouth now close to Matilda's ear. "I made them."

Matilda was uncertain that she had heard correctly. She shifted her weight awkwardly from foot to foot and waited for some sound to escape from between her lips but none did. The ceiling lights above her flickered momentarily warning of the library's imminent closure but still she found herself unable to respond to the information she had just received. It didn't seem to make any sense.

"You should see your face!" It was the woman again, her voice skidding off the library walls as she began to reverse the pram and then negotiate her way through the disabled side of the exit barrier. "I always love watching the reaction that gets."

Matilda scurried after her, glad to be out in open space where the salt air from the bay might clear away the confusion assaulting her befuddled brain. She could see that the woman had stopped a few yards further on, her backside half propped against a low wall while she bent to prise something from the tray underneath the pram. It was clearly some kind of album; square and large with a clear protective covering which she stroked lovingly before signalling for Matilda to come over and join her. Then sitting together on the wall the woman slid the book across both their knees and opened it up.

"These are the others," she said, carefully unfolding the tissued pages one by one. "Look."

Each page contained the photo of a baby. Some of them were beautiful like the ones in the pram but others were more foetus-like, the translucent blueness of their skin cold to look at as though they had recently been plunged into an icy bath. A few of them had their eyes open but mostly the images were of babies in sleep, their delicate lashes sealed tightly in innocent slumber.

82

Matilda studied the photographs carefully searching for any idiosyncrasies in the babies' demeanours that might suggest they were not real, but there were none. Each child seemed perfectly human and alive.

Finally, the woman beside her closed the book and clasped her pallid fingers together like a nun in prayer. Matilda could sense the rise and fall of breath easing its way from her companion's mouth and saw too that her eyes were closed, her body as still as the stone Buddha on Matilda's mantelpiece at home. The tide had begun to turn and with it a stiff sea breeze was curling its way up from the bay to tease at the women's hair and worry their clothes, but on they sat without a word. Only when the library had finally locked its doors and extinguished its lights did the woman stir, taking something from her pocket to hand to Matilda.

"My card," she said, her voice gravelled with breathing in the salted air. "Call me anytime." Then she released the brake of the pram with her foot and strolled off towards the town without looking back.

Sitting in the bus on her way back home Matilda's fingers nibbled at the card in her pocket, but she decided to look at it later after her mother had gone to bed. Her earlier encounter was not something she intended to share with anyone until she knew exactly what it was she was dealing with because those babies had undeniably wakened in her something quite disturbing.

The rest of the evening was spent preparing work for school and afterwards, when her mother retired, Matilda went to retrieve the card. She was surprised at how unremarkable it was.

Alice Goodchild. Born again babies, it read. Then a telephone number and that was it.

Matilda slept on her compulsion for three nights before making the call and even then her apprehension came close to stopping her dialling the digits. What kind of person would create pretend babies, she wondered? And what kind of person might even consider purchasing one?

For the first time in five years Matilda allowed a ghost from the past to slip through her carefully erected defences and thought about her own dead infant. Someone like me, she admitted sadly to herself as Alice Goodchild's voice spoke to her from the other end of the phone line.

They arranged a meeting for the following Sunday afternoon and Matilda spent the days beforehand searching for excuses not to go. But when Sunday came and the hundred or more reasons to renege still sounded unconvincing she found herself catching the busy bus into town and making her way towards Alice Goodchild's home.

It was not an unpleasant day, the leafy remnants of an early morning squall crunching agreeably under Matilda's feet as she walked and she was at her destination well before the allotted time.

The house was red-bricked Victorian, big and imposing and not at all what she had expected, although what she expected was not altogether that clear to her either. The garden had obviously been carefully attended to with a clipped privet hedge just low enough for Matilda to appreciate the old grandeur of the place and by the time she had negotiated the gravel path leading up to the front door she felt totally at her ease. Moments later the woman, Alice, had ushered her inside and they were standing together in a kitchen that could have been the size of Matilda's whole flat. Everything in the room sparkled with almost clinical cleanness, from the pure white finish of the units to the black granite work surfaces devoid of any superfluous dross, and the disparity between the building's outer shell and its interior took Matilda by surprise. The only evidence of clutter was on the walls whose every inch of space was invaded by a plethora of framed baby pictures; the subjects real or created, it was hard to tell.

Alice motioned for her guest to sit down and gestured towards the photograph album lying between them on the table.

"I assume the reason you've come is to have another look," she said, her eyes fixed on Matilda's as she pushed the album across the space towards her. "I can make you anything you like, although Middle Eastern is the hardest skin tone to get right. Saying that, you're hardly going to want anything but a white baby, am I right?"

Matilda tried to conceal her annoyance at Alice's presumptuousness but found herself instead nodding in agreement. There was something about the woman that she found disconcerting yet inexplicably the connection she felt between them made it difficult for her to get up and leave. So nervously she inspected the pages of the album for a second time, pausing occasionally to point out some small detail of endearment that moved her emotionally, a tiny tear at the corner of one baby's eye, a first tooth spiking its way through the lower gum of another. When she reached the last page there was only one issue that needed to be addressed, but Matilda was reluctant to bring it up for fear of being deemed callous. As it was, Alice made it easy for her.

"You're wanting to know how much each one costs?" she asked, not unsympathetically.

"Yes," said Matilda. "If you don't find that too offensive."

Alice's face remained impassive before she spoke.

"It's how I make my living," she admitted, "but it's also my vocation. Women contact me from all over the world because they've heard that I can help them. Women like you, I imagine, who have either lost a baby or who can't have one – all sorts. And the price? Well that depends on what you ask me for."

Matilda pointed at one of the babies on the wall. A boy. Cornflower blue eyes staring straight into the camera lens, a chubby thumb sucked between two fat lips.

"That one," she said. "How much?"

A pleasant smile emerged from the corners of Alice Goodchild's mouth.

"Three hundred, maybe a bit more," she said. "But you need a photograph to show me exactly what you're looking for. I can't go copying other peoples' babies now, can I?" She reached over suddenly and patted Matilda's hand. "It would defeat the purpose, wouldn't it?"

Matilda nodded her head, reaching to retrieve a worn leather wallet from her handbag and with the greatest of care slid out a small Polaroid snapshot from under one of its transparent pockets. The photograph had never been removed since the day she put it there nearly five years ago and even now she was reluctant to hand it over to somebody else. Noah had been only three weeks old when it was taken, his small body hammocked in the big strong hands of her husband, Joe.

Matilda's heart lurched and she fought to keep her emotions in check like she always did.

"Will this do?" she asked, handing the photo over to Alice. "It's all I have."

Alice inspected the baby's image with the meticulous eye of a plastic surgeon preparing for a complicated cosmetic procedure.

"He's very beautiful," she said. "I promise that I'll make a good job of it, but the devil is in the detail as they say. I'll get my notebook."

For the next few hours Alice scribbled her way through pages of information that, at first, Matilda felt uncomfortable about exposing. To start with it was about recounting physical features but later she relaxed enough to confide that both her baby and her husband had died together in a car accident. Alice, in turn, spoke frankly about how she had herself lost two children several years earlier. That had been the catalyst, she said, for persuading her to learn the skill of creating her reborns. She assured Matilda that, down to the last individual eyelash, her born-again baby would be a perfect image of the one she had so tragically lost and the final cost would be down to how much time Alice would have to spend on getting the baby's expression just right.

Later, as Matilda made the return journey home she could feel the shadows in her life evaporate as hope of cradling her baby in her arms again began to grow.

She did not speak of her arrangements to buy a pretend child with her mother whom she knew would disapprove and try to dissuade from the madness of it. Instead Matilda spent the following weeks trying to maintain an outward air of detachment from her newfound situation but daily being drawn to the high street baby stores that seemed to suck her in. Hour upon hour was spent in infants' clothing departments where she would mull over and finally purchase an abundance of the tiny outfits on display, happy to think that they would now never be outgrown.

Alice had promised to contact her within a month and Matilda did not put the time to waste, building up a wardrobe of garments any new offspring might be proud of. These she set amongst Noah's original clothing which had remained untouched within her wardrobe since he died.

When the phone call did eventually come it was not with the news that Matilda expected. Instead, Alice, whose tone seemed genuinely apologetic, said that she had succumbed to a particularly nasty virus and work on Noah had come to a standstill.

"I've been in bed for days," she admitted, "and I'm just not well enough to do him justice. I'm sorry."

Matilda didn't need to think about it twice. As soon as school was over she picked up a few basic groceries en-route and headed across town. It took Alice a good five minutes to answer the door and when she did it was obvious that the task of getting out of bed had been a huge effort. Globules of sweat sizzled over her hot cheeks and the whites of her eyes had been seized by brown spidery threads resonant of some South American tree toad.

"Bed," Matilda ordered, reversing Alice into the hallway. "I'll bring you something to eat. You look as though you could do with it."

Alice's begrudging legs carried her up the broad stairway, eventually disappearing from view through an open door on the landing. Matilda made towards the kitchen, passing on her way the big black perambulator that continued to accommodate the timeless babies inside, a reminder if she'd needed it, of her ultimate purpose in being there. She switched on the kettle and began to unload her few groceries into the fridge smiling when, from somewhere above her head, came the unmistakable sound of muffled snoring. She would let Alice sleep for as long as she could and then surprise her with a proper meal when she woke up.

Checking the contents of the fridge for something more substantial to eat and finding only her own meagre offerings Matilda looked about the kitchen. She scrutinised the room, searching for the source of the hum that teased her with its absence, and followed the steady drone to a small door hiding thief-like near one of the corners.

The pantry.

As she approached Matilda could feel its coolness seeping beneath the door to nip at her ankles, spreading upwards through her body like some involuntary stalagmite in an underground cave. The smoothed brass handle turned easily and the freezer's tenor hum filled the windowless space before Matilda managed to find a light switch and turn it on. She had found what she was looking for - the smart white chest occupying a good part of one wall.

With chilled feet Matilda shuffled forward until she could easily place her fingers under the rim of the lid to prise it open. It needed a couple of goes but eventually there was a slurp and the jaws of the freezer yawned wide to disclose its innards. Matilda's eyes strained their way through the haze in search of a ready meal that might be easy to defrost and cook but there was nothing to see except icy steam and two separate bags of frozen chickens lying together at the bottom.

She leaned in and picked the biggest one up, rolling it over in her hands to warm away the condensation that had gathered over its outer wrapping. For a chicken it was quite a convoluted shape and probably, Matilda decided, much too big to prepare before Alice woke up, so she reached in for the smaller one and swayed for a moment like a set of kitchen scales weighing one package up against the other. Then using an elbow to close the lid, she rested them on the freezer and fixed her gaze on the clear plastic, wet now with the heat of her hands. Some stray feathers still clung stubbornly to the plucked birds' pimpled skin and although it made her slightly nauseous Matilda bent closer for a further inspection.

That she had not realised her mistake earlier, seemed to Matilda afterwards, a sure sign that fate was trying to tell her something. Only when feathers melted into downy hair the colour of corn and pimpled skin had transformed into pink baby flesh did she acknowledge the gruesome truth of her discovery, but even then it took only seconds for her to come to a decision.

What did it matter, she asked herself, when in a few weeks' time she would be safely cradling a child again and her grieving would finally be at an end. No. She would never tell a soul. After all such a secret was a small price to pay for having a replica son of her own. Then replacing the packages back in their frozen tomb Matilda gently closed the lid.

She would go and wake Alice up. They would discuss any

final modifications necessary to make Noah perfect, as nothing less would be acceptable to her now. And later there might even be a takeaway to share if Alice was up to it.

It was the least she could do, Matilda thought, considering there was nothing in the freezer.

Man on a Corner

AFTER SIX WEEKS FRANKIE HAD EVENTUALLY worked out the sequence for the traffic lights. The knowledge of this held little significance to what he was actually there for, but it served to pass a bit of time on miserable evenings when the sky over the junction seemed to possess its privately owned bucket of piss. So far that was five out of the six weeks.

Normally Frankie Maguire wrapped himself up with the resolve of a naked polar bear as the slightness of his frame allowed for little ingress from the cold, and wet clothes invariably led to a spell indoors which did not go down well with the rest of the brotherhood. Anyone who could man the protest should man the protest, he'd been told, even though tonight that particular mantra seemed to have faded somewhat with him being the only one in attendance. Still, the evening had turned unseasonably warm giving Frankie the chance to offload the heavy jacket he was wearing and confirm his loyalty to the cause through the stories inked upon his skin. It irked him that the others, who normally gave him a ribbing about having Olive's name embedded in his knuckles, were not there to witness his allegiance in the more impressive works sheathing his biceps.

During his teenage years, a few decades ago now, tattoos had been something of a taboo form of self-expression, a permanent and grubby way to make a point even amongst the working class community where Frankie grew up. He remembered the first time his da had spotted the improvised bluebird on his forearm.

"You could at least have made it one of our flags," yelled his father during the pasting that had followed. Da had been a man with standards, standards that he expected his offspring to adhere to often through the persuasion of his fists. But Frankie never really let that get to him because once he learned that undersized men like himself could possess the belligerence of a pit-bull, he could exact his own standards right back. Yet when Marie, his daughter, arrived home recently with a series of delicate rosebuds braceleting her wrist he had let it go, for some things were worth fighting against and others not.

The lights at the corner of the junction blinked red, amber and green every few minutes, the ebb and flow of traffic somehow therapeutic in the dimming light of dusk. Once in a while a driver would honk his horn in support or more often wind a window down and shout obscenities into the coming night. That evening already there'd been one 'Wanker,' a 'Fuck you asshole,' and a 'Piss off and get a life,' but Frankie had stood firm, the pole of his flag steady in his fist, his head high.

Although he was missing the company of the others there was something noble in being able to stand there on his own and to remain resistant to the taunts of passing ignoramuses, for that is what he considered them to be. Besides, apart from the noise of the traffic and the insults being hurled his way, there was no better place for praying than where he now stood. It was certainly superior to the distractions that came with the constant thrum of machinery accompanying his working hours at the factory.

Praying was something Frankie did a lot of when he wasn't at his job. It was as though the grey matter in his brain could only function with a constant swell of prophetic words to feed upon. Olive commented on it sometimes when she noticed the sealing of her husband's eyelids outside of sleep.

"Frankie," she'd say, "all those holy words are going to burst right out of your head one day," and Frankie, most times, thought that she might have a point. Yet he could never rid himself of the need; not since what had happened to their youngest, Brian.

Not since his own faith had been tried to the limits and found wanting. Sometimes he spoke the words just loud enough for only himself to hear, *Jesus give me a break and take me away from this worthless life* or *Dear God, would you please just kill me as well,* but Frankie was not given much to worthless self-pity and he knew anyway that it would only add to Olive's suffering too.

She wasn't religious like him and he sometimes wondered how it was that she was so much better at managing her own grief. For Frankie knew that prayer was the only thing, the only thing, that made sense of anything anymore. That and in a lesser way, the brotherhood.

When he'd started going to the meetings it was just to get out of the house. And Olive had been brutal. "Look," she'd said. "Our Brian wouldn't have wanted to see you like this. Go down the Meeting Hall and get yourself some company Frankie. It'll be good for you." So he did.

At first, he'd been accepted not unexpectedly with a quiet sort of suspicion, although Frankie's own father had once been a stalwart of the community in that particular area of Belfast. But the old adage 'Like father like son' was not something greatly relied upon anymore and anybody recent to the brotherhood had something to prove.

"Yer da was a great man for the cause," was the hook and line inevitably cast towards Frankie during the meetings and his reply was initially something non-committal. Politics and what it did to people had long ago lost most of its attraction and had in fact doomed any relationship he ever had with his father, but gradually Frankie understood that to be fully accepted he needed to be seen to conform.

"Aye," he'd reply safely, "he was that."

Then one evening that seemingly harmless stance of impartiality was no longer an option. Frankie was trying to relieve his bladder in the toilet at the time, the urge to pee suddenly stifled by the unexpected company of a man shouldering him closely at the urinal, the flow from his penis undisturbed while Frankie's dribbled and halted like a tap with a faulty washer. If it was noticed there was nothing said but after shaking his tackle the man spoke.

"Well now, Frankie," he said, "it's about time you showed us some of your mettle. We need more boys to fly the flag these days." With that he zipped up his flies and left.

So that was the story – that was how Frankie came to be standing on the corner holding up a flag and identifying time sequences on the traffic lights.

After the toilet incident he'd volunteered immediately for although he wasn't exactly sure that he agreed with the cause anymore he thought it would do him good to stand up for something. He could always persuade himself that he was really standing up for his religion even though the actual flag thing was more his da than him. And if he needed a reminder of his own beliefs he had only to look at the *Jesus is my friend* and *God is Love* tattoos that now dominated both upper arms.

An hour and a half had passed since Frankie's arrival at the corner and with his legs numb from standing he tried shifting his weight about to alleviate the pins and needles that tingled his feet and were threatening to journey northwards. Without the other men there his noble stand had been okay for a while but now he was starting to feel faintly ridiculous. The words of a Script song that his daughter played kept running through his head - maybe he'll get famous as the man who can't be moved ... there are no holes in his pocket but a big hole in his world. Without the flag he would be like that song, he thought, and for some reason it made him think of Brian.

His son had been dead for fifteen months come the 21st of the one they were in. There was no explaining the terrible pain of it still, nor could there ever be for Frankie but time at least was making things seem less raw. Guilt, however, was something different and grew daily inside him like a silent metastasis already obliterating most of his vital organs. If Brian had been killed by a gunman, crushed in an accident or succumbed to a terrible illness, then at least there would have been someone else to blame. Instead Frankie was left with his own blame for not saving his son from the noose that stole his final breath.

Frankie tried to force himself not to think about it. He tightened his grip on the pole and swung the flag from side to side.

He tried to concentrate on the reason for being there but the image of his son on the end of a rope just wouldn't pass.

Why had Brian not talked to him? Why had that wee girl, pregnant as she was, not come to the funeral? Why had Frankie not realised his son's mental suffering and done something to help?

His heart was rung out over and over again at the thought of his own inadequacies. Olive had been more forgiving of herself but then you never really knew what went on inside people's heads. Frankie smiled sadly at the irony of that; it had caused the one and only row they'd had after their son's suicide.

"There was nothing we could have done to stop him, Frankie," Olive had said one night when they'd gone to bed and she'd had enough of the dark shadow continuing to veil their lives. "You've got to stop beating yourself up. Our son was lost to himself with the depression for whatever reasons. It wasn't our fault – not his neither, I suppose. It was just the black dog that got him in the end."

Thinking about it now Frankie could see that she was right. But at the time he could easily have shattered her skull against the wall and watched with dispassion as bone fragments embedded themselves into the plaster. It had been that bad.

He knew, of course, that Olive's grief was wholly as great as his own for she had borne their son and gifted to him that rarest of qualities, the ability to love without condition, while Frankie himself had bestowed only the misery of a melancholy soul. And now, standing there on the corner with his flag and his thoughts and a wretchedness that seemed to draw marrow from his very bones, he began to cry.

Without the pole to support him, remaining upright would have been impossible, so Frankie gripped on tight and through the wetness of his eyes he could make out the blurred letters of Olive's name, blue across his white knuckles. *OLIVE*, they said. *O LIVE*. Funny how you can look at a thing for years and never see it, he thought.

"For fuck's sake." The voice smashed through the sound of the traffic like a car crash. "Jesus Frankie, get a grip. We didn't think you'd take it that bad when we didn't turn up."

There were three of them, the man speaking, Gerry, walking slightly ahead of two others. They all laughed together. Frankie's eyes dried in an instant.

"Grit from the road," he said. "It's been annoying me all evening."

"Aye, right," Gerry said, stopping so abruptly that his companions slanted themselves like falling dominoes behind his back.

"We've been watching you, mate, from up there, checkin' you're doin' your bit for the side," and he pointed to a spot further on down the road. "You've not been doing much promotional work, have you?"

There was an edge to his voice that Frankie recognised from his da.

"I've been flying the flag, Gerry. That's what I agreed to do. I don't know what you mean by promotional work."

"Promotional work," Gerry repeated, "Y'know – letting the public know who they should be supporting. Making them feel safe to have us fighting their corner for them. Writing down the fucking registration numbers of the bastards who give you jip."

"I can't hold the flag and write things down at the same time," Frankie said, knowing that it sounded as pathetic as some school kid trying to be smart with his teacher.

"That's funny," bristled one of the other men.

"It isn't meant to be. It's true."

Frankie's own hackles had risen partly due to the embarrassment of being caught crying but also in response to the threat in Gerry's tone.

"Anyway," he continued, "why weren't the three of you here instead of playing hide and seek in the bushes?"

"You're a real fuckin' comedian this evening, aren't you Frankie," the third man said, his mouth distorted by the vileness of the words he carried in his mouth. "Maybe you think flying the flag's a fuckin' joke too."

O LIVE... O LIVE

It had been a sign. An epiphany.

Frankie could see it now.

"I don't think it's a joke," he said. "I just think that it doesn't really matter in the whole scheme of things."

On the road traffic continued to drive by and a van driver honked his horn while showing a two-fingered salute from behind the safety of his front windscreen.

"Better get your pens out," Frankie said. It didn't matter to him anymore what they thought, "seeing as I'm the one here holding the flag."

The force of the blow sent him back several feet into a fencepost shattering the wood and embedding the flagpole awkwardly between the connecting railings. He felt the slither of blood journeying from his nostrils towards his mouth, but he knew at least that they wouldn't hit him again, not in plain sight anyway.

"Now that's what I call fuckin' funny," said Gerry reaching to retrieve the flag and spitting a globule of green phlegm past Frankie's head onto the pavement, "and y'know, there'll be more of them jokes to come, mate, once we've reported back."

"I won't be protesting here anymore," said Frankie through bloodied teeth. "My family's more important to me than a friggin' flag."

The words were released more carelessly than he intended, opening a door for the verbal kicking that was to follow. The smallest of the men bent forward, his body language almost confidential, his mouth in close to Frankie's ear.

"Like your poncy son was important to y' Frankie, eh?"

Frankie tried to hoist himself up to sitting but there was an incredible pain beginning to chain its way along his vertebrae. He glared up at the three faces leaning over him.

"You keep my son out of this," he said.

"You're a pathetic wee bastard, aren't y' Frankie," said Gerry. "Not man enough to take a few home truths, are'y?"

"Maybe it's a case of 'like father like son'," said the third man. "Maybe poofters run in the family." He put one hand on his hip and flopped the other out in front of him like a dead fish. "So what d'y say, Frankie? Maybe Brian topped himself because of his big girl's blouse of a da."

Frankie knew that he should just let it go, that to retaliate

96

would only add to his own misery, but he couldn't. Yet the words that eventually emerged sounded as hollow as a blown-out blackbird's egg.

"My boy wasn't gay, if that's what you're saying. Sure his girl's having a baby."

But the men had already lost interest. Their sport was over for the evening, their minds set on reporting back a treachery that would undoubtedly merit a further list of consequences.

Frankie could only watch as they marched off, the flag in Gerry's hand flaccid as a useless penis against the pole, until they disappeared around the corner and out of sight. He leaned back against the fencepost to ease the ache in his back and closed his eyes. Nobody would come, not even the police who had probably caught the whole thing on CCTV - they were never going to intervene in a fracas that had its own agenda and thus ultimately its own reward. Even the traffic had eased and without the flag Frankie was just a sad - looking old drunk collapsed on the footpath.

Darkness was seeping up through the grey concrete, spreading chill through Frankie's small man bones until it reached the cavern of his skull. It stretched and probed until the space it found seemed filled with a strange clarity that hung there like a promise but would soon be vanished. Frankie absorbed what he could in the few seconds that he had – the futility of a worthless cause, the uselessness of regret, the utter sadness of lives half lived because of ignorance and spite and when he opened his eyes again it was to a new hope.

What if Brian had been homosexual, like they said, or the people from the other side somehow different from himself? Life, after all, was only a series of breaths. In, out. In, out. He would go home to Olive now and begin to breathe.

Perfect Imperfections

THERE IS A VOICE INSIDE US that lies hidden lest another sees the vulnerability of our soul. It begs to break the bonds imposed upon it by our compliance, but it is always there, present only in the deep recesses of our minds, like a heartbeat pumping, pumping, pumping towards extinction. The voice must always know its limitations and be content to simply be. But when the wind of change is set, it rises from its place of rest, tugging and pulling us with it as it goes.

And so it is. I only came to recognise it after you had gone.

The day we met was nothing more than any other day. Save for the lateness of my taxi there was no great sign to herald the event to come and I sometimes ponder how my life might be if fate had made me early. I was then a mere apprentice at my surgeon's trade, a young ambitious doctor whose arrival heralded no more than just a passing glance and I settled for a position near the door where an exit could be swift once my perfunctory duties were performed. Society parties, domain of the decadent and self-indulgent classes, were a necessary yet abhorrent chore to me and no less that day than any other.

Leaning lazily against a wall I thought to give myself some time for decency's sake, before making my excuses to depart. The room, crammed with nubile bodies, oozed with a familiar mix of energy and lust, but I knew it would not be long before the boundaries of propriety could be broken and the rules of that particular game would be upturned. I had witnessed it before and did not wish to be a party to it once again.

You were standing apart, resting your head against an open window and breathing in the dampness of a London street. I seemed to be beside you without thought or movement or endeavour and you held me thoughtfully with your eyes.

"You find me beautiful," you said. It was not a question – only a simple statement of fact.

"Yes," I answered, absorbing every nuance of your lovely face and all the while still unaware that the voice inside was stirring from its sleep. We left together hardly taking time to mingle either word or touch and you took me with you to your home.

"Love me," you said, knowing already that my heart was lost within those words and there could be no withdrawal. So I loved you then as though I had the world to give, and you in kind, repaid the giving of it many times besides. Our bodies met in one great crush of unison and the song we sang together echoed its melody out into a lonely city night. Afterwards we slept, entwined together by the other's love.

The dawn awoke me, shining silken threads of sunlight on your face and I marvelled at the stillness of your sleep. I traced a finger lightly across your cheek, feeling the sweet softness of breath against my hand, and I laid my head against the hollow of your neck and breathed you in. And that is how we were until the whispered voice began its discontented tune.

"Will you love me when my face is lined with age?" you asked, afraid, touching your flawless porcelain skin with trembling hands.

And thus began the litany of doubts I feared I could not counter or refute. The only certainty I knew beyond reproach was that I loved you then the way you were. Yet somehow you could never seem to love yourself or see your beauty through another's eyes and so the tiny imperfections in your mind became a portal to another world. The hungry mouth that once had met with mine in longing and desire was suddenly too thin, too average for your taste. The lines that danced around your eyes now proved to be an enemy of time.

And so the race you self-imposed commenced.

"A small correction here, my love?" you asked, examining your mouth with care. Then later, with your swollen pouted lips, you came to kiss me gratefully on the cheek. Those eyes that crinkled softly when you laughed took on a startled look of ageless wonderment, but nothing more. And your soft breasts, my place of comfort in the night, would soon become a frozen pillow for my head.

"I thought you beautiful before," I told you time on endless time, but nothing could prevent the great crescendo of your secret voice, released from all its limitations and now running free. If I were to live it all again, should I have held you gently in my arms and chided you for not believing in yourself, in me? Could I have then persuaded you to keep the voice at bay? Perhaps, I do not know but I, a willing perpetrator in the crime, was surely jointly bound to share the blame.

I wept the day I found you with another man and later when I asked you why, you turned and innocently asked, "Can you not see? To him I freely give my flaws without constraint, yet you and I must share the other's need. That is my special gift to you, my sweet; these perfect imperfections."

Your words had lain between us in the aftermath and though, in part, I understood your reasoning, I could not bear to face your honesty with mine, for it was then I recognised the voice that I had long misunderstood; it was my own. In life some moments stand alone in time, a metamorphosis of thought transcending any reason and only understood by looking back. Your nemesis and mine could only ever be explained in retrospect when finally we heard the voices sing as one in perfect pitch and left the shattered glass behind.

I wed a childhood sweetheart, as unlike you as any woman I could find. Her eyes perhaps were never quite as wide or wonderful as yours, her skin not just so flawless in its beauty or her mouth so sweet, but the inner voice was never on display to tempt and lure me as it had before. Instead, the changes that enveloped her came slowly, warmly welcoming the passages of time without the need of pure perfection.

And now, today, I see your face again, not standing by a window softly lit with dappled light or staring at me from the cover of a glossy magazine, but there in some litigious rag, as sad as any photograph could ever be.

I know you only by the colour of your eyes, as green as emeralds speckled lightly with their flecks of gold, but that is all. The face that once was chiselled by the finest surgeon's hands - my hands, is not a thing of beauty to me now but some pathetic caricature denying still the cruelties of time.

I cannot help but lay my fingers on the page to sense the frozen tightness of your smile and feel regret. I think of you, fresh faced and smiling up at me across a room of strangers long ago, the young ambitious model waiting, waiting for her knight to come and champion her cause. And there was I.

Tonight my driver brings me promptly to the door, his envy fiercely palpable beneath the grin. Too often he has seen me with the endless stream of wealthy clients seeking solace for their souls by beating back the ravages of time. The beautiful, the rich, the young, ah yes, the young of course, are here in salutary admiration for their god.

The room is smiling at me, faceless frozen smiles from people paying homage to their maker one by one. And so it is. The voice can never recognise its limitations.

Anyone for Dessert?

ELEANOR DUNNITT PUSHED HER BIFOCALS BACK onto the bridge of her nose and squinted to see better a house number on the invitation. There was none. Instead, at the top of the exquisitely hand-crafted card there was written only a name, 'Manor Lodge', and below, in smaller print, the road.

Instantly, Eleanor thought about those shops where if you looked at the price then you probably couldn't afford to buy the clothes and it was a bit like that with houses – if you had a posh enough name then you obviously didn't need to bother about having a number.

She thought about her own ordinary little semi with its unremarkable '25' nailed into the door and sighed.

It was a beautiful autumn morning and Eleanor didn't mind at all the walk along tree-lined avenues of weeping birches and copper beech trees. She had after all taken the day off work specially – a rare occurrence since her husband's redundancy six months earlier but it would be worth it. From the moment that she'd received the invitation she could hardly keep her excitement in check and it was important that she arrived at her destination smartly on the dot. Arabella Hunter-Smythe would not be best pleased if she didn't.

Arabella had a son in Eleanor's son's class and for some reason which was totally beyond the boys (not to mention their mothers) they took an immediate shine to each other. Giles Hunter-Smythe was a rotund little chap with fingers the shape of fat sausages, mischievous piggy eyes and a mass of sizzling red hair that sat suspended on his scalp as if there on a purely temporary basis. Jimmy Dunnitt, by contrast, looked as though he had been recently smoothed on his mother's ironing board. There were no angles on Jimmy and from his rounded silken-blond head to his extensive size ten feet there was a fluidness about him that reflected the affability of his character. Based on the principle that opposites attract, then Giles and Jimmy were in some incorrigible way, made for each other.

The same could not, however, be said for their mothers, a fact that Eleanor had recognised from the outset but chose to disregard for the sake of peace and harmony. While Arabella's speech contained a distinctive clipped Hampstead inflection Eleanor's northern tones sounded common in comparison. Her clothes, her furniture, her hair, her car or, for God's sake, even her husband, seemed inferior to that of the family Hunter-Smythe. Yet Eleanor could not bring herself to be covetous of their standing or possessions - it would just have been nice to be invited round a time or two but she never was. In fact today was the very first time in all the years of knowing Arabella that she'd been asked to call and although the event had been labelled 'ladies' lunch' Eleanor knew with certainty there would be some ulterior motive tagged to it that would in some way serve to reiterate Arabella's dominance over her social inferiors.

Turning a corner into Cedar Falls Boulevard, Eleanor at last arrived at Manor Lodge's imposing entrance gates and with one final panicky glance at her watch (she was one minute late), skittered the final few yards across the gravel and up the steps to the front door. Arabella was there waiting for her in the porch.

"You are a naughty girl," she admonished, pointing a perfectly manicured forefinger between Eleanor's eyes. "We'd practically given up on you darling but come, come, lunch is being served!"

The 'we' had already established themselves around an enormous oval table in what was obviously the dining room. Two vacant seats remained – the hostess chair near the patio doors and another beside the large antique dresser at the back of the room. Eleanor's shoes clip clopped like one of the Billy goats gruff as she dashed across the parquet floor and sagged into her seat. A woman opposite smiled thinly but continued to chomp on a bread stick and there was a disconcerting 'ping!' as Arabella struck a spoon on the side of her wine glass to signal that proceedings were about to commence.

"Welcome my dearest friends!" she announced abruptly, gesticulating wildly with both her arms. "Welcome indeed to my very humble abode, but before I wish you Bon Appetite I have an exciting announcement to make. My darling boy Giles has this very week been accepted into ..." there was a dramatic pause, "Habbernabber's School for fine young gentlemen!"

Eleanor felt the palms of her hands smacking off each other as she joined in the polite applause around the table. So that was it then, she thought, poor Giles is to join the ranks of the elite to be groomed for a life of one-upmanship or petty superiority.

She sat through the first and second courses of how the poor boy would now mix with aristocracy, become an overnight millionaire and possibly slay every dragon in the history of mythology and Eleanor's desire to take revenge began to grow.

It was then that her attention was drawn to an array of desserts neatly laid out on the mahogany dresser nearby. A crystal bowl of fresh fruit salad, strawberry pavlova and a pyramid of plump profiteroles drenched in a rich cascade of chocolate sauce. Wonderfully tempting, every one of them. Eleanor had a very sweet tooth and eating something naughty might just help to dispel any uncharitable thoughts towards Arabella so she continued to stare at the profiteroles until there were specks before her eyes which made her blink. In fact it was only one speck, but quite a large one that hadn't moved when Eleanor reopened her eyes so she tilted her head to peer a bit more closely. And there it was - its little spindly legs firmly rooted into the thick solidified chocolate - a bluebottle the size of a man's thumb nail. It stared at her with its unseeing blowfly eyes because it was quite dead and Eleanor returned its stare with a mixture of compassion and envy. The poor thing must have taken a while to die, she thought, but death by chocolate - what a way to go.

Meanwhile Arabella was instructing her kitchen staff to clear the table in preparation for the final course. Her voice was becoming ever more animated with the excitement of the occasion and Eleanor had overheard the words 'piece de resistance' mentioned a couple of times. Without pausing to think she leapt up from her chair and grabbing the pyramid of profiteroles exclaimed to her mystified audience, "To our wonderful hostess Arabella we thank you for this truly momentous luncheon. It seems fitting that she should be the first to sample the results of her unselfish labours preparing these wonderful desserts. May I Arabella?"

Arabella's face was flushed with smug supremacy. Eleanor had had her uses as a dumping ground for Giles when an unexpected round of golf was on the cards but she never expected the mother of that ghastly boy Jimmy, of all people, to extol the virtues of her culinary talents.

"Why how very considerate of you, Eleanor," she purred back. "By all means. Absolutely."

Eleanor smiled sweetly as she returned the plate to the dresser and carefully prising the top three profiteroles from their perches dolloped them in the middle of a waiting dessert bowl. She felt guilty for what she was about to do and taking one last apologetic look at the unsuspecting bluebottle forced its iridescent body deep into the creamy centre of one of the pastries before discreetly extricating her thumb with a gentle shlurp. Then slowly with the measured step of a warden accompanying some prisoner to the gallows, she made her way to the head of the table and with a modest, "My pleasure Arabella," placed the bowl on the table and resumed her seat.

After the meal Eleanor excused herself early with the pretext of having to visit a sick relative which was, of course, a lie but she needed time to walk off all those puddings she'd been scoffing earlier. What a pity about the profiteroles, she thought - they were always a real favourite of hers but still, she'd had more than enough fruit salad and the pavlova had been utterly mouth-watering.

Arabella to everyone's surprise had refrained from sampling any more of her desserts and was decidedly quiet for the remainder of the meal. It was somewhat out of character and a number of the guests noted with concern that she had gone quite blue in the face at one stage.

As Eleanor retraced her steps along the boulevard she felt the afternoon sun seeping into her back giving her a decidedly warm feeling inside. Copper beech leaves crackled and scrunched on the pavement under her feet and the sound brought a sudden smile to her lips. For everything needs a little bit of crunch sometimes, she thought. Absolutely.

Any Ordinary Day

DAYLIGHT FINALLY RESCUES ME FROM THE secret corners of sleep that have eluded me in the night. Outside my father's footsteps scrunch across the gravel as he leaves for work but I remain completely still, strangely connected with the newness of another day and the whispering of spring that it brings.

This morning, though, there is a strange reluctance in my bones to stir and I do not want to go to school. For the life of me I cannot tell you why, for really I do not know myself.

In the room next to mine I can hear, through the thin partition wall, my younger brother wrestling with the demons in his sleep. Sometimes he cries out in the middle of the night and I listen for my mother's hushed reassurance as she comforts him, gently exorcising the bogey men inside his nine-year-old head.

Nobody knows the source of his unhappiness so they buy him things to try and compensate – computer games with 18 years and over discreetly positioned on the back side of the box in tiny print. He plays them unconstrained inside his room when he comes home from school but the violence amuses him, he tells me, so I choose to leave him be – he is my little brother after all.

I dress and go downstairs where in the kitchen Mum is washing dishes while humming her oldie songs into a sudded sink. The smell of burnt toast begins to irritate my nose. I eat breakfast and run.

107

My friends are waiting near the entrance to the school chattering on about their weekend escapades and flirting unashamedly with boys from the year above.

I notice Janice Tilley hitching up her skirt to knicker level and most of the other girls follow suit because in order to avoid detention it is always best to flaunt the rules in the safety of numbers. My own skirt remains glued fractionally above the knee for, much as I would like to conform to this rebellious act of unity, I do not wish to display the course hairs that lurk darkly behind my adolescent thighs. Neither do I wish to give to Archie Bannerman further reason to expand his cruel observations to every other boy within our class.

We snake begrudgingly through the gates and on towards the main assembly hall where Miss Higginson, our vice-principal, scans her prey with the shrewdness of a jessed hawk. The boys form in orderly lines, by year, on one side of the room; we girls along the other and, in between, the monitors feed their superiority upon a hoped for dissent among we, the lower ranks.

The wave of hush comes always as a shock. I watch rows of heads in front of me bend like young, winded trees as pupils shift their weight tediously from foot to foot. Today's sermon is about to start. Janice Tilley nudges me gently with her hip and a low sigh squeezes from the side of her mouth. We have both heard it all before.

"Children!" Miss Higginson begins and the staff sitting in a row of chairs behind her jump. "This morning's assembly is dedicated to one word and that word is deference." She pauses then for effect, her eyes blazing like the night-sights on a hunting rifle searching for a target in darkness. The lines of trees ahead of me are suddenly stilled and nothing stirs. Miss Higginson carries on, "Treat others the way you would have them treat yourself and you will ultimately reap the rewards in later life. If you show other people respect you will be repaid for it tenfold. And if you demonstrate deference, yes, deference, children, you will find that adults will return your obsequiousness in kind."

I think it would be a lot easier just to say, "Try to be nice to each other," for at least then the younger pupils might understand but I have long since lost the will to comprehend how the minds of adults work.

When the bell finally calls us for the start of classes we file out through the big doors as submissively as cattle in an abattoir would resign themselves to their brutal and unalterable fate. Another day at Memorial College has begun.

Janice links my arm, hauling me along with her towards the lockers to collect our stuff. She likes my plainness which is no threat to her and I am useful for my status with the teachers. Yet there are times, if she knew it, when I would gladly give to her my conformity in exchange for a single day of her rebelliousness. But today my usefulness has little weight.

At the lockers a young teacher whom I do not recognise is taking names into a book. The book has pretty, glittered swirls across its cover and I imagine it to be meant for something other than to list the names of unruly girls who keep their skirts too short, but it is not.

"Do you not know what the school rules state?" yells the teacher into Janice's face, a spray of spit freckling over my friend's cheeks. "Get that skirt pulled down to the proper length and report to the office at break for blatant flagrancy of uniform rules."

I wonder if she has been to assembly earlier and if the word deference is in any way within her remit. She redirects her eyes to gaze at my compliant skirt length. I almost wish she'd pick on me as well, but instead of that she simply nods her approval. Respect, it seems, is reliant on certain rules that only adults are allowed to generate. She turns on her heel and strides away.

"Bitch," breathes Janice, at the same time tugging on her hem with one hand and giving a fingered salute with the other. Then nonchalantly to me, "See you at lunch then, Melissa," and she slopes off up the corridor while I mount the stairs to the next floor and my first lesson of the day.

Within my head there is a beat. It is attached to the fingertips of my teacher in room fourteen, science block and it is relentless. The beat pounds persistently as fingers hit wood - dadada, dadada, dadada - rather like the thud of machinegun fire I hear from my brother's play station in the bedroom adjacent to mine. Jesus, I think, as if it wasn't enough to listen to at home.

Mr Hamilton teaches us biology and he is beautiful. His hair is the colour of honeyed corn and when it flops across his eyes he deftly flicks it back again with fingers that no science teacher ought to own. They are a piano player's fingers and I envy their soft delicacy when I compare them with my own stumpy appendages. In short, my teacher is what we teenage girls describe as 'fit' and I'd actually quite fancy him myself if only I wasn't female.

Mr Hamilton, you see, sadly isn't into girls or so I hear. Daniel Gregson tells a good story about it most lunch times in the canteen but I notice that this morning his chair is empty so we must forego the daily diatribe of faggot jokes until his return.

I sit at a window seat. It is my reward for being obedient and conscientious. Daniel, on the other hand, is always forced to sit right up at the front near Mr Hamilton's desk where he can be ogled at or leched after depending on who you like to talk to. I rather suspect it is the latter. I think about what Miss Higginson was on about this morning and consider what kind of reward Mr Hamilton might reap from his so-called deference towards vulnerable pupils like Daniel. These thoughts are running through my mind as the register is being called.

"Bannerman."

"Yes sir."

"Craig."

"Present sir."

"Gregson. Daniel Gregson."

Silence.

"Where's Gregson this morning?" Mr Hamilton enquires of the class, his face struggling momentarily to hide its disappointment.

"He's absent sir," somebody says.

And so it goes on.

Outside in the teachers' car park a stray dog pees up against somebody's shiny hubcap and then trots off indifferently out of sight. Along the pathway leading up to school pretty yellow and purple flowers dance under an April sun and the fresh green of spring filters through the new leaves of an overhanging beech tree.

Ours is a well kept school. This is just an ordinary day.

"Wilson!"

Nothing.

"Melissa. Pay attention. I'm calling the register." Dadada, dadada.

"Sorry sir. Here sir," I mutter apologetically seeing his mouth betray a smirk he usually reserves for the other girls. The drumming stops abruptly. Mr Hamilton checks his watch and the lesson begins.

"Okay everyone. Turn to page fifty-two. Chapter six. Photosynthesis. All eyes down."

Something flickers across my field of vision. It feels like the briefest flash of light on metal and I turn idly towards the window again to try and locate its source. Unexpectedly I see Daniel Gregson ambling nonchalantly up the gravel path, a golf bag slung casually over his shoulder, silver clubs glinting sharply like staccatoed bursts of sunshine.

"Jenkins, can a plant photosynthesise without light?" asks Mr Hamilton from somewhere near the back of the room but I am only half listening. There are more intriguing things to observe through the windowpane and Daniel, with his long, easy strides, is making surprisingly good ground. Soon enough he will reach the big double doors at the main school entrance but now he is just close enough for me to examine his face. He looks quite relaxed, happy even, and the corners of his mouth curl gently upwards into a warm smile. I half expect him to look up and see me watching him but instead he reaches an arm effortlessly behind his left shoulder and pulls out one of the clubs. I can see now that it is an odd shape; that it is perhaps not a golf club after all. I suddenly do not dare to wonder what it is. And I don't want to be in school today.

From my mouth comes only silence. From my eyes a terror that chokes its way through my uncomprehending brain and buries itself deep into my consciousness. Only my ears function with a sweet clarity.

Dadada, dadada.

In a terrible unison timed like the opening bars of some Beethoven concerto the gunfire rings out with the first awful screams. In the room where I sit though, everyone has petrified themselves to stone, their legs reluctant to accept the urge to flee; their brains as yet too stunned to function normally. Even Mr Hamilton is rooted to the spot, unable to fully comprehend the battle raging through the corridors on his behalf and fleetingly I pity him for his ineptitude. But Daniel now is on his way to reap his rewards. I let myself imagine him reaching the bottom of the stairs and then I time the steps it takes for Daniel Gregson to arrive at room fourteen.

Nine seconds. Ten. Eleven. Three more and still my body refuses to move from its privileged position beside the window.

Dadadada. Dadadada. Dadadada.

The volleys of gunfire are deafening and brutal but I am like Lot's wife pillared in salt and cannot join the other pupils now lying prone across the parquet floor. All I can do is look into my teacher's disbelieving face for one last time before the quiet opening of our classroom door. And there is Daniel, smiling now his sweetest smile as he prepares to take the final shot.

Just like the play station guy, I think and wonder why it is that anyone should be so surprised.

Towards the Light

CAL DISCOVERED THAT IF HE SQUINTED hard enough from under his eyelids he could detect the edge of his lashes shivering like cobwebs in frost. Like the ones he saw too in the further distance where the corner of his bedroom walls greeted the ceiling in a confusion of curling wallpaper and furred damp. Steady streams of frayed light tumbled unchecked through the window onto his bed, seeping into the duvet to embrace him with their indifference.

"Calum!" It was his sister barking from the kitchen. "If you want a fucking lift then get down here."

His mother would never have used language like that to get him up. She would have rapped cautiously on the bedroom door and peeked through the slit to waken him gently. But his mother had died nearly a year ago and with her the soft corners of his life had somehow also managed to evaporate.

Cal punched the pillow into his ears and concentrated on his lashes. He counted a dozen or more spidery tendrils before the pain in his eyeballs forced his lids to finally seal and then he focused on some funny little floaters within the blackness. Anything to avoid the day. Anything to re-route the inevitable consciousness of time.

Cal felt the house shudder with the sudden vicious slam of a door conveying his sister's departure. She would remain as mad as hell at him until her return later but it was worth her anger just to have won the silence. Its isolation found him welcoming and compliant, and he sucked in breath over and over until beneath the covers there was only stale air in his lungs and cobwebs within the chinks of his eyes. And for a brief moment in Cal's day he tried to love himself.

Love was not something much discussed within the walls of his home. Even when his mother was alive it was an emotion rarely voiced but this Cal had understood knowing as he did the price of defying the wishes of her husband. For once Cal had heard his father telling her, "You've turned that little sissy into a real mummy's boy. Stop petting him, for Jesus' sakes woman, and let him stand up for himself."

After that his mother was cautious about outward shows of affection towards her son and demonstrated her love for him in ever subtler ways. He might find a little book of poetry or stories hidden beneath his pillow for she knew how Cal was addicted to both or he would discover money secreted in his blazer pocket for sweets. But as the pain in her bones like a silent shadow overcame her so too did those acts of affection diminish until all that was left was a skeleton walking and a boy's abandoned heart.

Cal thought of these things now only fleetingly for there was a day to confront and he dared not dither longer in bed. In any case his sister's exodus posed now another problem - that of getting to work on time without a lift. So, wearily, he stretched his long legs over the side of the bed while his feet searched for the reality of a cold floor.

The kitchen clock was announcing the hour when Cal sat down for breakfast. The eighth and final chime sounded as he prepared his cereal but, late or not, he would never leave home without something in his stomach. It was a rule his mother had insisted on and he rarely objected as it ensured some precious moments in her company. But this morning he was thinking not of her but of his father who would return home soon from a night shift. Cal wondered often about his father. It was not that the man meant to treat him cruelly, for harsh as his words might have seemed at times Cal recognised they came from a desire to toughen his young son up. No, there was something else that hung between them like an unspoken accusation lingering in the dead ends of their conversations.

At first Cal thought it might be because his parents had deceived him, that he had in fact been swapped at birth or adopted even, but then he found his birth certificate in a shoebox under their bed. Afterwards he was never quite sure whether what he felt was relief or disappointment in discovering that he was his father's son after all.

As he chomped through his cornflakes Cal studied the four yellowing walls of the kitchen. The sepia colour they had become seemed almost fitting given their propensity for storing the past. All that information they'd hoarded over the years, all those unanswered questions embedded inside their soured plaster. If he were to dismantle the walls brick by brick Cal thought he would surely find a truth selfishly concealed within every one and he wondered how he'd ever managed to extricate the straight facts about anything.

"Why's Mum lost so much weight?" It was a question he'd asked more times than he could remember. And someone would mutter that a virus had stolen her appetite or she'd gone on some weird grapefruit diet or even (only half jokingly) that a tapeworm was more than likely munching its way through her insides. But meanwhile the bricks in the walls would be sheltering their secret truths that tapeworms and grapefruit and viruses don't take away someone's soul as well as the flesh upon their bones.

At twenty past eight Cal washed, dried and cleared away his used dishes. Then passing the hall mirror he carefully checked his reflection before leaving the house and hurried down the road where Saturday morning traffic smooched by as though relieved to have left the stresses of a working week behind.

At the bus stop Cal waited anxiously and prayed that the bus would arrive soon. He needed to be on time as decent weekend employment for school kids was hard to find and he had always thanked his luck for having somehow landed the job in the first place.Today though, the number twenty-six was pulling in to disgorge a handful of passengers, the familiar phlut and hiss of the suspension announcing its arrival at the stop. Cal jumped on board, paid his fare and sat in the first unoccupied seat. Only then did he reach into his jacket pocket for the small anthology of sonnets that would occupy his thoughts during the journey.

Carefully he opened the book at a marked page and began to read, *"Since there's no help, come, let us kiss and part; Nay, I have done, you get no more of me, And I am glad..."*

"Hey Caroline!" The voice was shrill and girly but a boy's voice all the same.

Cal kept his eyes focused on the poem and concentrated hard on the words, *"And I am glad, yea glad with all my heart..."*

"Hey sweetie – come on down and talk to us and read us a fairy story." Staccatoed laughter repeated between the seats like machinegun fire. "Let's see how you swing those hips Caroline!"

In the mirror fixed to the driver's cab Cal had a clear view to the rear of the bus where several boys from school were thrown together along the rear seat. All stared towards the back of his head as though attempting to bore a voodoo spell into his skull. He returned his attention to the book's open pages but where there had been words was now a series of woolly black indecipherable lines shifting with the movement of the bus as though siphoned through an old movie reel. They flashed inconsistently across the field of his vision. White and black, then back to white again and for no reason Cal could properly understand he felt the sudden searing guilt of missing his mother.

At the shopping mall a few stops later the boys got off, wolf-whistling their passage to the exit before showing him the finger from beyond the window pane and it was hard for Cal to imagine that once he had believed them to be his friends.

He remembered a night after the death of his mother when they had enticed him to vandalise cars down the estate, how someone had shoved a baseball bat in his hands, how the crunch of wood splintering on metal had excited and sickened him all at once. And how, even when he'd been taken down for questioning at the police station and come home afterwards expecting his father's approval, there had remained lingering between them that same sense of disappointment and unease.

Cal realised then that whatever alien and threatening thing

116

that lurked within him would never be accepted or forgiven by those whom he cared about the most.

But now the bus was snaking its way out of town where graffitied walls were replaced by hedges of clipped privet and where houses wore an air of undisputed superiority. At the stop nearest the golf club Cal got off and began to run, up through the arched gateway and along a broad avenue to the clubhouse, then round to the tradesmen's entrance at the back. Somewhere close by, a church clock was peeling in the ninth hour of the day...

Late in the afternoon a group of players were gathered expectantly by the big open windows overlooking the first tee. Cal's gofering by then had been constant and relentless throughout the day and finally Gerry Dennison, the club pro, called him over.

"Right son," he said producing a small silver key from his pocket. "You've earned it today, alright. Follow me before the light fades too much." The two made their way to the changing room where from a locker Gerry extricated a set of clubs and handed them over. "You're sure you're still okay with this arrangement Calum?" Gerry asked, aware that the boy's partial payment for a day's work was unorthodox and probably not entirely legal.

"Your coaching is the best wages I could get Mr Dennison."

"And there's nothing else?" probed Gerry, sensing in Calum's demeanour something uneasy that he hadn't noticed since the kid started with them.

"I was just wondering how come you got my number that time," said Cal who for some time had been itching to ask but felt he couldn't. "You know, to offer me this job here."

It had been six months since Gerry had taken him on and the surprise was that it had taken so long for the kid to finally enquire.

"My brother watched CCTV footage of you down at the station son," he confessed. "He said if you could swing a club as sweetly as you swung a baseball bat then I'd better be the one to know about it."

"Uh-huh?"

"And he wasn't supposed to but after he'd interviewed you he passed on your number and the only way I could get you to come was by offering the gofer job. I had a pretty good idea that you'd take to the game once I'd got you here. "

Cal stayed quiet, taking in the words that for the first time since his mother's death actually made him feel valued by another human being.

"You don't think I'm useless then?" he asked, holding tightly the older man's gaze.

Gerry steered the youngster outside and together they approached the green where an ambered sun was scattering its light upon a gathering dusk.

"You're nothing short of a genius with a golf club, son," he said, inserting a ball onto the tee. "Just believe and you'll discover that for yourself."

Cal squinted hard from underneath his eyelids, focusing on the tiny fuzz of white beyond his feet. He felt the easy swing of his hips as he connected with the ball and watched it slice the fairway, disappearing out beyond the waiting void. To a place where a boy might finally love himself, he thought.

If only he believed.

Tomorrow is Another Day

THE ROOM IS DARK. OUTSIDE, THE light of a new day has not yet managed to penetrate through the dusty windows of the schoolroom and the shadows inside seem somehow stuck in some kind of time warp. For every day it is the same. Every day the gloomy shadows lie unmoved on the classroom floor and every day I sit on my crossed little fingers wishing I was anywhere but here.

This morning I am crouched in the corner, knees hunched up near my chin waiting with the others. We have been permitted to come inside only because of the relentless freezing rain outside but it is no place of comfort. I wish with all my heart that I was wet and cold in the playground and far away from that witch they make me call 'teacher'. I hate her. I hate her beautiful yellow hair and her red lips and her white teeth. But most of all I hate her eyes because they have always a hard, mean look in them that big people don't seem to see at all. Only we children seem to see it and I often wonder how that can possibly be.

She is coming now. We can all tell when she is coming. Clip, clop, clip, clop. As she advances along the corridor her high heels make a sound like one of the Billy Goats Gruff crossing the bridge. But she is not one of the greedy goats. She is the Troll underneath the bridge. A happy thought. The Troll gets itself killed and I imagine a dozen different ways for the Troll to meet its end.

"Sit!"

How can a word hold such menace when it has three letters and only one meaning? It is one of the many words that she has honed to a fine art and we have learned to recognise the more dangerous ones. But it is her tone that acts like a warning siren to the inevitable eruption to come. Just a slight sharpening of the voice that builds to a crescendo of hysterical rants and accusations about how we are all savages and worthless Cretins. I think I know what a savage is but have no idea at all about the meaning of Cretin. I guess it must be something pretty awful. I make sure that, even though I am a savage, I am an unobtrusive one. That way I can get to go to the toilet in the middle of class sometimes.

Today I ask out with a look of desperation on my face and with knees squeezed together for effect. She lets me go because she does not like the thought of having her classroom messed up and I am jubilant as I escape down the corridor. It is my way of getting one over on her. Inside the toilets I go straight to the wash-hand basins. Above one of them is a peg with my name on it and hanging neatly below is my drawstring wash-bag created from the remnants of my mother's old dress. I pick up the bag and press my nose firmly into the material to smell the familiar scent from within. I feel the outline of a little bar of soap inside and the squashy facecloth that has been cut from some old towel from around the house. It is my one and only connection with home and my only means of surviving the school day.

As I return to the classroom I notice with a heavy heart that the rain has turned to sleet and there is no possibility of freedom now. I cannot even feign illness for I know that as much as my mother loves me, she would never allow me to miss a moment of school unless I was at death's door. I sometimes think that being at death's door was preferable to being in the witch's coven. I re-enter the shadowy world that she has created for us and get through the rest of the day as best I can. There is no laughter and no fun and everything I have learned will be forgotten because it has been learned under threat and duress.

When the final bell rings we line up like soldiers on parade and are frog- marched to the school gates where we are handed over into the care of our waiting mothers. The witch stands there beaming at them, her teeth sparkling and yellow curls springing up and down on top of her shoulders. Only the eyes remain hard and unyielding in their coldness but still the big people do not see. It is a mystery to me.

My mother takes my hand and inquires about the kind of day I've had. If I could make her see. If I could only believe that she would understand. But because I am just a child, a savage and probably a Cretin, I remain silent and trudge wearily home.

Tomorrow is another day.

At the Gate

THE SIGN ON THE GATE READ ' Groups only please. Sorry for any inconvenience.' And that was it. Mohammed leaned his back against one of the pillars and yawned. He had arrived there fifteen minutes earlier and was now becoming bored with the wait but knew he had no choice.

The sky was an azure blue. Cloudless. And the air around him was as clear as the desert night through which he had come. Silence encompassed him but he did not mind, for it was a welcome relief from the constant drone of engines in the evening sky and the ceaseless thud of bombs as they hit their targets.

Mohammed Aziz. Beautiful boy. Fourteen years this spring and the neighbourhood's star soccer player. His skin was the colour of rich honey and it was glowing now with sweat as his eyes began to take in their surroundings with more care.Those eyes. Not brown as you would expect but the darkest, deepest green you could imagine.

"You will have your choice of any girl," his mother told him proudly every day, but he was too modest to believe it and too busy playing football to think about such distractions.

Twenty minutes gone. Surely someone must come soon. It was pleasant sitting at the gate in the peace and quiet but it would be nice to have company or even make up a group to go in together.

Something stirred. At first Mohammed sensed the faintest whisper of a breeze as it caught the black curls on his forehead and cooled his brow. Then came a rush of warm wind racing up through the blue and settling with a final whoosh somewhere near his feet. He looked up. There they were not six feet away from him, standing together. The girl spoke first.

"What's that sign, Mother?"

"I can't read it from here but the gate looks as though it may be locked. Perhaps there are opening times that we didn't know about."

"It says that we have to go inside in groups."

Mohammed's voice was clear and distinct as he got to his feet. They turned to look at him.

"Who are you?" The girl was close now and scrutinising his face.

"Mohammed Reza Aziz. And who are you?"

"Jennifer. What kind of a name is that? Mohammed. It's not an English name."

"It's an Arabic name actually. Mohammed was our Prophet, so it's a very important name."

Jennifer stared at the boy who was not that much older than herself and awkwardly stuck out her hand, "Pleased to meet you Mohammed Reza Aziz," she said and they both smiled shyly.

Jennifer's mother looked tired. Her face, normally settled in a kind of vague gaze, was pinched and drawn with worry.

"I need to let your father know, Jennifer. He should be home by now and we need to tell him."

Jennifer stared at her mother and said sadly, "Someone is bound to tell him, Mum. Stop worrying. Everything will be fine."

Mohammed could sense the rising panic in the woman's eyes and without thinking took both her hands in his. Ruth looked into the green eyes and saw only her reflection. It was as though this child, a stranger to her, held her life inside of him and she felt oddly calm.

"I am Ruth," she said simply.

The three sat together on the grass, none of them speaking and each content to harbour their own private thoughts. Jennifer broke the silence first.

"So where is your mum, Mohammed?"

It came as a shock. He had not wanted to think of his mother yet. He did not want to voice his concerns.

"She is at home, I think," was all he said and Jennifer knew enough to leave it at that and move on.

"Do you think we'll have much longer to wait or might they let us in, just the three of us?"

"They have rules, Jennifer," replied Ruth. "We must abide by them and be patient. It won't be long, I'm sure, before someone else comes."

They did not have long to wait. There was no great whoosh of wind this time, only a sense of tension in the air before he finally appeared. Introducing himself loudly as 'Steven Jeffers' he strode confidently towards them hesitating only when he spotted the boy.

Mohammed eyed him curiously. The man's face was unfamiliar and he wore a strange grey uniform.

"What's with the sign?" The question was directed at no-one in particular and demanded little response, for Steven Jeffers was already rattling the locked gate impatiently. "Has anyone rung the bell?"

"There is no bell," replied Jennifer who remained seated on the grass, "There's just the sign."

Steven was unprepared for the delay but shrugged his shoulders and decided to join them on the grass. Ruth was regarding him with renewed interest for she had a cousin in the Air Force and recognised the uniform.

"You're a pilot," she said.

"Yes ma'am. I flew my last mission this morning."

Mohammed waited patiently. He was in no hurry. There was still plenty of time. He closed his eyes and thought of his mother and the feel of her arms around him as they huddled together in their small home. He thought about the plane that seemed to be closer than all the others and the sound of the missile searing through the night sky seeking out its target. He thought about his pounding heart and his mother's terrified sobs as their house imploded around them, but most of all he thought about the man he did not know who surely could not have understood the terrible destruction he had just created.

Mohammed opened his eyes and watched as the tears began to stream down the pilot's face.

"I'm really sorry, kid." Steven made no attempt to hide his distress. "It wasn't meant for you at all. I made a mistake. It happens sometimes."

Ruth reached for Jennifer's hand and held it tightly. They looked from the face of the boy to the face of the man and waited. Mohammed sat motionless, soaking in the confession that he had known would eventually come.

"You have done a bad thing, Steven, but that does not make you an evil person and I have already forgiven you," he said calmly.

Jennifer stared at him. She could not believe what she was hearing and her voice was filled with disbelief as she whispered, "He killed you, Mohammed. How can you forgive like that? I don't understand."

Mohammed simply smiled.

None of them moved.

They sat there on the grass waiting for the disturbance of air that would herald the arrival of another to their group and Steven, with the keen eyes of a pilot, saw him first. Far in the distance, a particle of dust transformed itself into a man who bore down on them with great speed. Closer and closer until Jennifer could finally focus on the features of his face. Closer. She knew the face now. Still closer. It was right in front of her. She could see him through the windscreen of the car.

And then nothing.

Ruth placed a hand on her daughter's shoulder and shook her gently. "Look Jennifer," she said. "He has come."

The man stood before them nervously. It had been a difficult journey, made all the harder in the knowledge that they would be waiting for him at the end of it. Ruth suddenly felt a great sadness, for she had wished with all her heart that he would not have had to follow them there.

Beside her, Jennifer thought about her father who would only now be hearing the news of their deaths. She thought of the years that she would never have his love, or a boyfriend's affection or her own children's devotion and she turned to watch the man who had taken her future away from her. He seemed disinterested in the gate and stood watching her closely.

"Was it lack of sleep or too much alcohol maybe?" she asked, needing someone to blame, as if in some way it might make things easier. He looked back confused. "It was the dog. I didn't want to hit the dog."

Jennifer saw the sorrow in his eyes and recognised that his pain could only be relinquished by her forgiveness. The delicate thread between life and death that connected them was hers to sever or strengthen as she chose and she now understood how easy it had been for Mohammed earlier.

"Will you come through the gate with us?" she asked the man and placing her hand gently in his, felt the squeeze of acceptance as they moved forward together to join the others. Ruth put an arm tenderly round her daughter's shoulders and fixed her eyes on the path ahead which lead through the now open gate. The pilot and the boy followed their steps in unison as they walked easily together behind the others.

They reached the gate and each of them paused for a moment to remember a life left behind to which they could never return. Only Mohammed glanced back for one last time, smiling in the knowledge that his mother had never come. Then they walked forward together, hand in hand, as the gate closed firmly behind them and the azure blue stretched out into an endless sky.

End of Summer Blues

HE DESPISED THE OLD. IN THE estate where he lived they ogled him through smeared window panes or netted curtains frayed with apathy and age and he sensed their eyes sucking his youth like wrinkling sponges as he passed. In summertime they sat on graffitied benches spitting crumbs of conversation through their yellowed teeth or toothless gums. But Ricky Platt had learned to keep that loathing to himself and satisfied his resentment by filching after dark and hawking worthless booty to his mates the following day. Sometimes he could hock a watch, a ring, a picture frame perhaps, but mostly the stuff was just tat that nobody cared about and he'd end up slinging it in the canal. Old peoples' things were just like them; worthless, obsolete.

She was spotted getting on the number twenty-two to Tannaghmore on one of his afternoons mitching school. Her back had an unmistakable camel-like hunch – that landmark of oldness he found so abhorrent, yet in her demeanour there was something unexpected that he couldn't put his finger on.

On a whim Ricky followed her onto the upper deck and sat two seats behind, lighting up a fag before his backside connected with the shabby blue upholstery. Inhaling sharply, his eyes focused on the back of her head where silver curls moulded themselves neatly round the contour of her skull. Like kisses, Ricky thought, and he noticed she had tiny ears.

She got off where open fields broke free from the confines

127

of city conurbation and he watched her disappear between two ivied pillars as the bus moved off. There was a thrill to following her that Ricky did not dare to confront just yet, but it amused him to think of the randomness of his selection that day and spying on her had been easy after that.

When he couldn't afford the bus fare he'd go on foot, setting off early to arrive as she fed her cat, emerging from the house with a tentativeness he began to find almost endearing.

"Here puss, puss!" he'd hear from his hiding place behind the garden shed. The weather had been kind, dry at least, and warm after the sun slid round the side of the house in the afternoon. In fact, Ricky was well pleased with his hideout and after the initial days of apprehension wondering if the shed was ever used he began to relax, realising that the garden wasn't attended to in any way.

Some days he sat there for hours studying her in the sunroom with her knitting, but he was never bored. There was always something about her that intrigued and irritated him like when her lips moved in silent conversation even when he knew she was alone. It had taken only a few weeks to become familiar with her movements, how she always drew the downstairs blinds at dusk, or the days she went into town for groceries, or her visits to the mobile library and local butcher. He began shadowing her with ease in the knowledge that she was too preoccupied with something inside her head or too senile to be aware of his presence.

After a month, curious to hear more of her voice and challenge her powers of observation, he'd even dared to instigate a conversation during a bus journey out of town.

"You want to sit here, missus?" he'd asked after beating her to the last seat a few minutes before.

She looked back at him stupidly then and accepted with a weak, "Thank you dear. You're very kind."

But it was pathetic how naïve she seemed and Ricky fought to hide the irritation at her gullibility, retaliating with his first forage into her domain. When she'd left the house one afternoon he let himself in using the keys that were dangling obtrusively from the lip of the coal bunker and it was as easy as that. A moron could have done it. But the first time was the best.

Adrenalin surged through Ricky's veins like electricity threatening to overload his naturally vigilant state of awareness. And it felt different from his other break-ins. Before it was grab what you could and scarper, not like some of his mates who stayed long enough to piss their names on the carpet and got themselves caught for the privilege. No, for reasons he could neither comprehend nor care about Ricky was suddenly measured in his approach and took the back scullery first, staking it out like a crime scene and walking the grid like he'd seen them do in those murder investigations on the TV.

A Belfast sink, its drainer lined with shiny empty cans, stood lonely against one wall while the worktops stretched their way nakedly around another two. It was nothing like those oldies' houses Ricky had seen before, so full of useless belongings gathering nothing but disgusting grime and he felt suddenly a surge of pride. Not for himself but for her and her unexpected disparity. Yet in the room there was an iciness that bit raw into his bones and after twenty minutes he left the same way he'd come.

From then on Ricky created a mental timetable in his head knowing that by the end of the summer he'd have covered every room. Tuesdays and Thursdays, the days she went to town, were good for detailed forays when he could take better cognizance of his surroundings. After the scullery came the hallway, the breakfast room, the lounge and then four bedrooms and a bathroom upstairs. Sepia photographs in dustless frames dotted the walls of each room, but there was surprisingly little else of notice except the constant cold that followed Ricky everywhere he went.

The sunroom he purposely left until that final day – a grand reward for his tolerance throughout the summer when he could have done the place over a dozen times. For Ricky knew that everything of worth would be in that room as sure as she would disappear to town at one o'clock and return again at five to knit and mumble into empty space.

She left punctually, boarding the bus at ten past one, and for the last time Ricky grabbed the keys and let himself in. His trainers crackled across the lino floor of the scullery until they met the soft familiar give of carpet in the hall. Out of sight a clock ticked its heartbeat through the innards of the house to match beat for beat, the throb of anticipation in his chest. Twenty seconds and he'd reached the sunroom door. A dozen more and he was standing in the centre of the room, an unexpected rush of heat hitting him like hard rain striking concrete down the estate and it struck Ricky that she'd put her whole life's warmth into that one room.

For a moment he simply stood and welcomed the intrusion to her world, so different it was to looking in, so much more intimate than he ever thought. An ancient telephone, its curled flex knotted erratically round the receiver rested on a table with her knitting, and in front of her chair the indentation of two tiny footprints had worn her presence into the carpet.

He scrutinised the room for signs of cash she was sure to have secreted over time – a bulge beneath the carpet, a tell-tale peel of wallpaper at a skirting or, most pitiable of all, a sweetie jar that might be stuffed with banknotes under the brandy balls that she squirreled away.

For an hour or more Ricky sweated vainly for his expected rewards until at last, angered by his thwarted efforts to uncover her Aladdin's cave, he paused to contemplate a retribution fitting her deceitfulness. Beyond the steamy windows of the sunroom his eyes were vaguely focused on the shed outside and then from nowhere she was glaring at him in the glass, her hands suspended weirdly in some mid air salutation that he failed to fully comprehend.

The hatchet connected with Ricky's neck in one clean sweep of the blade. She had not anticipated felling him from behind like that, but her reflection in the window had proved an unexpected gift of sorts which made the whole thing easier than she thought. It was amazing how she'd reeled him in, contemptible little bastard that he was. God how she despised the young and their stupidity although she knew she'd probably miss her summer's entertainment for a while at least.

The scarf that she'd been working on lay undisturbed beside the telephone and as she picked it up his prize began to flutter from the neatly pleated folds like crumpled ticker-tape around the room. She'd have to clean the mess up later on, but now there was a job to finish off before the sun went down and she could finally draw the blinds.

At last the familiar feel of the wool trickled its way lovingly between her fingers and she began to knit.

Nature's Way

THIRTEEN YEARS. THIRTEEN YEARS OF A memory lying dormant and extinct through the passage of time. She liked to think of it like that; all practical and matter of fact, fitting neatly into the packaged little compartments of her life where the luxury of self pity merited no place at all.

Then quite unexpectedly and with unforgiving harshness, those carefully constructed defences of hers shattered, exposing a vulnerability which lay gaping and sore like some open, maggot-infested wound.

He hadn't meant anything by it, of course. It was just one of those throwaway comments from a stranger that would normally have merited only a passing quizzical glance but her heart, which had been for so long steady and strong, had felt his words like a physical blow.

"It must have been nature's way," she overheard him say to his companion as they stood shoulder to shoulder with her on the tube and there was such sadness in his voice that she feared he might actually start to cry.

She was tempted to reach out to touch him in some act of recognition for his pain and tell him that she understood, but the doors of their compartment flew open suddenly and he was swallowed up by the sea of faceless bodies overflowing on to the platform. He would never know the effect his words were to have on her.

She never imagined that the trigger could be so inane. In fact, unlike so many incidents in her past where she wholly expected a backlash later on, the events of thirteen years ago had always seemed totally and absolutely laid to rest.

Until now.

The shock of it spread its tendrils into that dark place in her mind where the memories had been so meticulously buried all those years before when she and her husband had been married for only a year.

The news of her pregnancy had taken them both completely by surprise and there followed row after row about the sacrifices that would have to be made at a time when their careers were just beginning to take flight.

"How could you be so irresponsible?" he accused her when she admitted missing one of her pills. "We can't afford to have a baby yet."

And she knew that he was probably right. There was, of course, no talk of abortion but it was clear to her that the pregnancy was as unwelcome to her husband as it was a gift to her. Unlike some of her friends, who had been nauseous and miserable in the early stages of their pregnancies, she had felt amazingly energetic and healthy. The first time she felt the little hiccup jumping in her stomach that was the baby's kick she was beside herself with joy. What did it matter, she thought, that her career was put on hold for a while when the developing life inside her was beginning to make its presence felt? Yet she needed to be convinced that her husband, too, would really welcome this baby when it arrived and achieving that was not easy.

Before the pregnancy, when they had returned home from their respective jobs at the end of the working day, they sat and shared stories, commiserating and laughing together into the small hours. She had always believed that theirs was a combining of two souls forever connected, even if it seemed like a ridiculously childish and innocent notion. Even now she knew that he still loved her but it was as though the knowledge of the baby had somehow extinguished the fire in him that he had hitherto saved only for her and night after night he stayed later at his work until she could no longer bear the hurt of his rejection. Finally, on a day when she had been uncharacteristically plagued with backache, she confronted him with her anger.

"You're nothing but a selfish bastard," she was screaming when the first real stab of pain clenched her stomach and she felt the sticky wetness of blood trickling down between her legs.

On the way to the hospital she would not allow herself to believe that she might lose the baby but her husband, sitting next to her in the ambulance, was emotionless and unspeaking. Later in the evening, after finally being settled in the small private side ward, she watched him retreating through the swinging doors and out into the night. She believed in her heart that he was sorry for their loss although he did not speak the words. Those same words would remain unspoken in the intervening thirteen years as though the miscarriage was something that had never even happened.

When the lights of the ward were dimmed she made her way to the bathroom, taking with her the bedpan that had been given to her earlier by one of the nurses. Quietly she opened the door and perched it on top of the toilet seat. While the minutes passed she sat there welcoming her discomfort in the knowledge that her pain might in some way lessen that of her unborn child, and when it was over, there, in the lonely, nothing world of a cardboard bedpan, lay the tiny foetus. Then washing her hands carefully she pulled the door softly behind her and did not look back. On the way past the nurses' station she remarked with some embarrassment that she may have left something behind her in the toilet. And that was that.

Next day, the D and C to 'clean everything out' as they so coldly put it, was straightforward and uncomplicated. In only a few hours her husband would arrive to take her home again and life, as they had once known it, would be resumed with renewed vigour and enthusiasm. After all, it was nobody's fault and might indeed have been only for the best; a sentiment the consultant had reiterated during his rounds that morning when he remarked, "Try not to be too upset about it, will you? It is just nature's way."

It had not destroyed her life. There had been two other children, lovely boys, both healthy and beautiful and totally irreplaceable but she had been left with a feeling that she had not been allowed to grieve properly for her first baby who had been so easily flushed out of her life. In the end, though, she had to let it go and bury the dark thoughts before they destroyed her, as she knew they ultimately would if she let them in.

Now, as the tube hissed its way to a halt into her stop she could only wonder at how utterly bereft she felt. Never before had she allowed herself to even question what her baby would have been like had it had the chance to live. Would it have been a girl or a boy? Did it have blue eyes like her own or were they hazel like her husband's? Questions that would forever remain unanswered and as she stepped on to the escalator she felt the tears begin to flow as she wept for the years of guilt that had been so carefully buried with the memory of her first child.

Emerging from the cold, dingy world of the London underground she made her way across the busy streets towards the Embankment and finally down to the riverbank. There, stretching out before her, were magnificent clusters of golden celandine somehow surviving, against all the odds, the grime and filth of the city.

Carefully she began picking a handful of the little flowers and forming them into a neat bundle within her fist while the water lapped softly near her feet and the seagulls overhead squawked their forlorn cries into the wind. Deliberately, one at a time, she tenderly plucked a flower head from its stalk and tossed it into the flowing water. Then she watched as the thirteen perfect golden splashes of sun floated sadly away from her down the river and out into a lonely sea.

Non-returnable

LITTLE IN THE BRUISED HOSPITAL AIR offered comfort as the doors to the cancer ward slapped their familiar defiance in my wake. The unforgiving odour always caught me out and like a child crossing her fingers I held onto my breath, hoping to avoid that invasion of blued-blackness into my lungs like the disease cosseting my father further down the corridor. I stalled then and blew hard on my nose, irrationally inspecting the invisible aftermath on a deteriorated piece of tissue – madness, I thought. It was amazing what the inevitability of endings could do to your mind.

I didn't and never would admit those feelings to him, of course, and by the time my reluctant feet had found his bedside my face would show to my father a calmness which belied something rather different. Witnessing someone I loved gradually degenerate piecemeal in front of me was not something I'd taken to that easily. Brown eyes widened and folded again at my arrival.

"Good to see you love," he announced brightly enough, and then powerless to resist the now daily ritual, "Any news yet of me getting away?"

Slender fingers raised themselves from their resting place only to flop back again onto the white sheets, the physical effort of such a little thing telling in its simplicity. I was glad that he didn't have me fully in his sights, my deception too obvious in my look, if not altogether hidden within my reply.

136

"Soon, Dad," I lied. "They say you're doing well and hope to be letting you out before long." And pulling up the heavy visitor's chair I sat as close to him as I could while the slippery stained plastic sucked already at my warm thighs. "How's the pain?"

Through the blue transparency of his eyelids came a brief flicker of annoyance, but from the corners of his mouth where white spit settled, there twitched something of a smile.

"What pain?" he shrugged and I loved him for that - that ability to wring the devil out of everything bad. It was a quality I thought he had passed on to me but lately it was little in evidence and I was feeling the rawness of my own inadequacy.

"Tell me about the children," I heard him say, "and Tom. How are things going with the business?"

"The kids are fine - settled back into their uni terms again. They ask about you, you know. In fact they chat more to me on the phone now than they ever did when they lived at home. It's a hard one to come to terms with, really."

He smiled then - genuinely, as though identifying with some funny little joke that I hadn't realised I'd made.

"That sounds about right," he said. "So, Tom?"

For an hour or more I answered his questions about the family and my work and his plans for when the doctors would eventually come to their senses and let him out. He was expecting a visit from the consultant, he said, and was sure he'd be having a weekend at home in next to no time. When I left, that infectious optimism of his was still buzzing its way around my head but in my heart the tainted air of inevitability had already begun its suffocation. I got into the car and drove home.

The house was deep in sleep when I arrived or so it always seemed since the children's departure and a late afternoon light still hung on to the day. Yet winter would not be denied its share of gloom and with darkness only a touch away I skulked from room to room filling the house with artificial brightness I did not myself feel. In the kitchen I examined the contents of the fridge thankful that the remaining pre-prepared bag of salad had not yet cannibalised to inedible mulch, and set the table.

He arrived home from the office earlier than usual. Tom, my thirty-year long husband, was looking unusually relaxed and communicative and we sat down then to eat.

"How's your dad today?" he asked, a limp leaf of rocket slipping from his mouth back onto the plate. "Any better?"

"He thinks he's getting out."

"And do you think it's fair that he doesn't know?"

The tone was unexpectedly accusatory and hostile although his eyes remained focused firmly on his food.

"He's my dad, Tom. Would it ever occur to you that it might kill him to know?"

"Well, it's going to kill him anyway - not knowing, isn't it, Jen? You're the one who's always been big on the truth."

Neither of us spoke after that although I knew he was probably right. It was just such a hard place for me to go to when I already had the guilt of it in my hospital-bruised bones.

Later in bed, I snuggled up tightly into his back where we had for over thirty years fitted so easily together and muttered, "Sorry" into the hollow between his shoulder blades. But the wheeze of his snoring told me that he had long since fallen asleep.

Next day I visited my father again. The lift up to the ward moaned under a weight of strangers, their mingled breath a mere fleeting connection with each other until they arrived at their selected floors. I got off with an elderly woman and a child whose thin arms shocked their way out from under her sleeves like some hastily created scarecrow. She skipped happily ahead of us, the heels of her socks half way up the back of her legs, before the woman called to her, "Sophie, wait. Your mummy might be asleep, now don't you be barging in on her."

So much sadness, I thought, so many people with lives full of shitty stuff that was far worse than mine could ever be and yet it was no consolation to me then. I turned sharply into the side-room that was my father's. He was sitting up, his body oddly askew against the pillows and I thought at first that he was in an awkward sleep. His eyes, though, opened as I approached the bed, the dark - mooned irises tracking my movements while I sat down until finally his gaze fitted into my own.

"You're happy, Jennifer," he said and I knew straight away that he was referring to me and Tom, so I nodded my head in agreement. "You met your matching heart when you met him, didn't you?" he went on, the sentimentality of his language coming as no great surprise for he had always loved to challenge words in a way few others could. "And you're happy?" The sentence rose like a question this time, his need to have things confirmed to him now more difficult to conceal.

"What's happened, Dad?" I asked and in the asking was overcome with a dread that made the words choke within my throat.

He sighed; a long, sad whistle of a sigh before speaking, "I've had a visit, just after you left yesterday - that Mr Gerard, the consultant, along with his entourage. Kids, most of them, in spanking new starched coats that matched that same starched look they had on their faces. And he told it to me straight, right in front of them and that lovely wee nurse who's been so good to me, that it's the end of the line - for me, anyway."

There was no blame in the way he said it, only a resignation in how he looked at me, as a faithful dog before being put down would look for one last time towards its trusted owner. And for a long while after that he just cried.

Tom was home from work and had made the dinner when I later arrived back at the house. For the first time in weeks he didn't ask immediately after my father instead persuading me to sit down straight away to eat while he served out the meal. There was an odd, slightly frantic manner about him that I hadn't witnessed since the beginnings of our relationship when those same qualities had been enough to lure me in. And I wondered when it was that he had lost them or if it was me who had, without knowing, simply stopped taking any notice. He waited until we'd finished eating to tell me, quite brutally, I thought afterwards - like the surgeon's knife slicing its way through unsuspecting pinked flesh, like some indifferent doctor disclosing to a patient that their cancer was untreatable.

"Jen," he announced. "I think we ought to talk."

I suppose I shouldn't have been surprised, for after all I had long since been aware of the distraction in his look and the apathy he seemed to shoulder whilst in my company.

"Who is she?" I accused, my voice suddenly struggling for purchase in the sullen air that hung between us, "Anybody I know?"

"Does there have to be someone else?"

"There usually is."

"It's nobody," he said, looking straight at me in a disappointed sort of way. "It's just us and what our lives seem to have become. There's no excitement; no pleasure in it anymore," adding almost indifferently, "the truth is, I think we haven't really loved each other for a long time now and you just haven't wanted to see it."

A sour surge of bile spiked the back of my throat as I fought to take in his words. "So what are you actually saying, Tom? That you don't love me anymore? Out of the blue. Just like that. No fucking warning at all. Is that it?"

I stared at him across the table steeling myself for the battle ahead but all he said was, "I simply hoped that we could try to be what we used to be together but I don't think that's possible now. Neither of us seems to be able to make the effort."

With that he reached over to skim his lips across mine before disappearing up the stairs to find whatever solace he could in sleep.

With the strained light of dawn struggling to nudge through a chink in our bedroom curtains the telephone rang. It was a nurse from the cancer ward asking me to get there as soon as I could; my father's condition had worsened overnight.

Tom drove us there in silence, neither of us prepared to re-visit that dark place of the evening before and knowing anyway that there were more urgent crises now to consider.

The lights to the main ward were still dimmed on our arrival and making our way quietly towards my father's room we were met by the pretty fire-haired nurse to whom he had grown so attached. In the uncomfortable awkwardness of her manner I saw that we were too late.

"I'm really sorry," she whispered, touching my arm and glancing nervously across at Tom, "but your father passed away a few moments ago."

If I'm honest, I think that all I felt then was relief. Relief at not having heard my father's dying breath or having witnessed that final moment of human consciousness which I knew to others could provide much comfort. I had never had the desire to be there for that and I was certain - nor would he have wanted me to be. But there was anger and frustration too that the opportunity to say goodbye should have been taken from me so cruelly and I vented my feelings on the nurse despite the trail of tears that had begun to filter over the pink apples of her cheeks.

"What the hell happened?" I asked coldly, approaching the lifeless corpse of my father who had been hastily laid out on the bed. "He was in great form when I left here yesterday."

The lie came out with ease, my need to apportion blame overriding any sense of fair play and Tom's look held such contempt that I half wished I had died along with my father.

"It's hardly her fucking fault," he said, and turning his back on me he walked off into the new day.

For some time I simply sat holding my father's hand, those long fingers of his shocking me suddenly with their inertness. I scrutinised the picture of his life within the lines that shot in random cuts across the pale, soft palm and wondered if a fortune-teller, yesterday, could have prophesied his destiny. Alive one minute, dead the next; surely no one could have predicted it happening like this – no one, I thought, except perhaps the doctor who had filched all hope with his cruel truths and left a man with nothing in his heart to beat for.

An unfamiliar nurse looked in, telling me to take the time I needed but hinting too that there were necessary regulations to be adhered to. I nodded in acknowledgment and longed for Tom's return but he didn't come back and for the first time it occurred to me that perhaps he never would. So it was in this new solitude that I would finally come to realise my failings in our marriage and view my husband's charges of complacency in a different light. There had been a cruel truth in his words and although my love for Tom was undiminished I began to feel his loss and was ready to accept my part in it. Such knowledge saddened me more even than the touch of my father's gradually stiffening appendages.

After they had come to remove the body I collected up the few belongings remaining by the bedside. There wasn't much; the only item of note a tired copy of Dickens's Nicholas Nickleby marked out with fragments of torn hospital newspaper. Like an accordion I allowed the pages to unfold, stopping randomly when I glanced some dialogue shakily underlined, 'Don't leave off hoping,' it said, 'or it's no use doing anything. Hope, hope, to the last.'

The words merely confirmed what I already knew, that my poor father, when all hope had been taken away and the truth finally exposed, had simply decided to give up and die. Then with only the last traces of his scent to comfort me I fled the room.

Outside the hospital entrance, where it was possible again to fill my lungs with unspoilt air, I paused to gather myself. It would be necessary to return later to finalise funeral arrangements, of course, but now I had a desperate need to seek Tom out.

Visitors hunched their way past, faces marked by where they had already been or where they sought to go and silently I said for them a little prayer. Only then did I notice, a short distance away within the Perspex shelter of dressing-gowned smokers and hospital staff, my husband shrunk into a corner like some lost child, his bent head belying a beginning baldness I had until then been unaware. My heart stuttered suddenly, touched that he should have changed his mind and stayed around for me after all when I had foolishly succeeded in convincing myself that our marriage was lost.

My feet began taking me towards the dingy shelter where inside a man, propped up by his mobile drip-stand, dragged urgently on a cigarette while a pair of hospital porters demolished their hastily smoked butts underfoot before slouching back to work. I noticed, too, a nurse standing in profile close to where Tom sat, the now familiar auburn curls flopping carelessly over one eye. Then with obvious tenderness she stooped to place a tender kiss on top of my husband's head, holding her mouth against his hair as though tasting his scent for the first time. And like an intruder witnessing some illicit yet fascinating tryst I found it hard to finally look away.

In the taxi the driver mercifully abandoned his patter after a few minutes and observed me only with his eyes from time to time in the rear-view mirror. I silently promised to tip him well when I reached home but meanwhile there was much to think about; a funeral to be arranged, a death to mourn, relatives to contact with the sudden news.

And afterwards would come another ending too; already I could feel its cold beginnings taking hold, for there was no returning it - the truth.

Or so I have been told.

Fallout

IT HAD BEEN A BUSY EVENING in A and E when they brought her in and he was upset that it should happen right at the end of his shift when tiredness was threatening to overcome him and he was already feeling mentally exhausted. He watched as the paramedics bulldozed a stretcher through the double doors and immediately recognised the mane of chestnut curls spilling out from beneath a hospital blanket. Sighing, he turned and followed them into the emergency room.

Although he had been a fully qualified doctor for more than ten years, he could not remember having to deal with a situation which affected his professional judgment. Certainly he had known many of the patients who had been wheeled through those same doors, but somehow he had always managed to remain impartial with regard to their medical treatment. Yet now, as he began working to try to save her life, he only felt inadequate.

As they moved her near lifeless body across from the ambulance stretcher onto the hospital trolley he listened attentively to the ongoing assessment of her condition from one of the paramedics. He had not needed to be told that it was drugs related. She had already arrested in the ambulance and it was only through the skill of the medics accompanying her that she had survived so far. A syringe was still attached to the vein in her heavily scarred forearm that lay motionless at her side. But much more shocking to him was how dramatically her face had changed. The cheekbones that had once been such an intricate part of her beauty were now protruding under skin stretched as tight as an over inflated balloon. There were deep lines etched beneath her eye sockets which themselves threatened to disappear completely into her skull. Only her lips were as sensuous as he had remembered them, but even they had taken on a bluish tone which contrasted with the pallor of her skin and made her look like death itself.

He could not comprehend how it could have come to this. Whatever road she had travelled in the years since they last met must have taken her towards some kind of hell which had no return.

He remembered how she had always pushed back the boundaries in everything she did, but that had always been part of her charm and attraction. She was an aspiring model when they first met and could have had her choice of men yet she had chosen him over the rest - for his kindness, she said. Now he felt that his kindness could only have had a hand in her destruction because it had allowed her complete freedom from responsibility.

At first she thrived under his protection and they had somehow managed to balance each other out - he, with his grand philosophies and gentle understanding of other peoples' needs, and she, with her free spirit and unfailing need for adventure and risk taking. For a while, then, they had allowed themselves to believe that their lives could be forever entwined and they fed on each others' diversities, but eventually her need for change became too great. Gradually, the qualities that she had cherished in him became the cause of her growing resentment and she walked out without even leaving a note.

He had forgiven her, of course, because in his heart he believed that she would someday return and he immersed himself in his work and waited.

Occasionally there were rumours of her drunken binges and outlandish behaviour in the local clubs and he knew that one day when he was working, she would probably arrive with some alcohol related injury. But he was not prepared for this.

He wondered at how any human being could allow themselves to lose their dignity in that way. The stench of urine hung on her trousers and the vomit that had choked her whilst in some drug induced state earlier stuck to her tee shirt. Her body was so emaciated that when he lifted her wrist to feel for a pulse, it was like touching a child's little delicate hand and he knew then that she was beyond his help.

They kept her alive for two hours. There were brief moments when it seemed as though her will to live might overcome the inevitable consequence of her self- inflicted abuse but it did not happen. In the end, her body had been ravaged by the drugs for so long that she paid the ultimate price. He called the time of death at two thirteen am and went in search of her parents.

He found them in the relatives' room, waiting anxiously for any news that might give them hope. They were embarrassed at first to meet him again after such a long time and under such circumstances which had not made it any easier for him to break the news. Later, driving home from the hospital he thought about how he had handled it. To be told that your only child had died was cruel enough, but to know that her death was sordid and degrading was simply too hard to bear. So he had described how beautiful she still was with her chestnut curls and her green eyes. He said she had suffered no pain and had spoken of her love for them moments before she died. He knew that by the time her parents were allowed in to see her she would have been cleaned up and they would never have to know.

Finally, he let himself in to his apartment and sat down slowly on his leather sofa. Reaching across the coffee table in front of him he opened the small antique box that she had given him once for some special occasion. Carefully he spilled the contents onto the glass surface and began creating little lines of white powder with his credit card.

It had been his only solace since she left him and as he snorted his first line he thought how very sad it was that after all the waiting her eyes had never opened. Then slowly he drifted into euphoria and none of it really seemed to matter.

Say Goodbye

A STALE SMELL OF SMOKE AND body odour lingered strongly in the office air. Detective Inspector Helen Lucas could feel it permeating her clothes like the slurry that seeped into the fields close to her home. She could never quite get rid of the smell of it in her nostrils. This was the floor of a working office, normally bustling with busy people but empty now and uncharacteristically silent. She had purposely chosen a time when the team had packed up and gone home, before performing this most cruel of all duties.

Helen paused in the middle of the room and looked around her. The walls were crammed with maps and pictures, pictures and maps. They were everywhere, vying for space amongst other innocuous details that pertain to the scene of a crime.

She fingered the tiny metal key that lay within her pocket. It did not feel cold to the touch but reassuringly warm and familiar and she began to make her way to a small private office in the corner where a name plate on the door read, "Detective Chief Inspector" in tarnished gold letters. Some joker had erased the "i" in Chief and it momentarily made her smile.

The door was closed but unlocked and it swung open easily at her touch. Inside, the room was in darkness save for the peppered shafts of light thrown in from a nearby streetlamp. The distinct smell of cigar smoke and whiskey still remained, as though waiting for someone's permission to finally withdraw. The past few days had been difficult for Helen Lucas, but no moment seemed as difficult as this. In the whole of her working life all she had ever aspired to become was a police Chief Inspector. But not like this. Not under these circumstances. There was no glory in it now or pride in her achievements and she fought hard to stay in control. But there was still a task to complete and Helen knew in her heart that no-one else could or should, be the one to finish it.

Sitting down quietly at her predecessor's shabby oak desk, she placed her hands on its smooth worn surface. She could feel a kind of connection and it gave her comfort to feel the warm wood beneath her fingers. The fading light was making it almost impossible to see now and Helen flicked the switch of the lamp in front of her, suddenly illuminating the only other object on the desk; a photograph in a most delicate filigree silver frame.

Now this newly appointed Detective Chief Inspector looked down at the two drawers beside her, one fitting snugly beneath the other. The top one was slightly smaller and more used than the other judging by its battered and broken handle which almost came away in Helen's hand when she tugged it open. As she looked, she thought it could almost have been her kitchen drawer at home such was the disorder and disarray of its contents. Some pens, a pair of broken spectacles, the top of an old whiskey bottle, a discarded ink cartridge and a newspaper article, crumpled and torn - just bits and pieces of a person's life. But what an extraordinary life it had been.

The man who had sat in that same chair before her had enjoyed an exemplary career. Having begun his police service as an ordinary copper on the beat, he had worked his way up through the ranks to become one of the most respected and decorated figures within his profession. But years of dealing with the most heinous of crimes had taken a heavy toll and on the final day of the trial of his last case where the defendant had inexplicably been exonerated he had gone home, put a gun in his mouth and pulled the trigger.

Here in his office surrounded by the smell of him and the feel of his presence it was impossible to believe that he was not coming back. The little bag they had given her to put his personal effects in seemed ludicrously inappropriate and she angrily filled it with his things. Pulling the drawstring tight, she placed it carefully beside her on the floor and reached in her pocket for the key.

The second drawer was no such open house for the curious and had always, to Helen's knowledge, remained securely locked when not in use. The key fitted uncomfortably into the lock as though unwilling to be party to any disclosure of its contents and it took Helen several attempts for it to open. As she pulled the drawer towards her, her heart began to thump relentlessly in her chest and it was with some effort that she placed a hand inside to retrieve the four items it held. Each one was carefully labelled and numbered according to who they had belonged to and where they had come from. They were as familiar to Helen as any of her own possessions because for some months she had been part of the investigating team accumulating evidence.

On the day the suspect was arrested she had been the one to find a small hidden bundle of belongings linking the death of the four victims together. Trophies, the bastard said, to remember them by.

Helen touched the little bell that lay before her and ran her fingers along the red silk ribbon by its side. She stroked the lovely flower head and tenderly held the Polaroid snapshot of a young girl. These once beautiful, personal treasures had been tainted and contaminated by a murderer's touch, but all had been deemed inadmissible as evidence because of some absurd technicality which ultimately allowed a sick, psychotic killer to walk free.

It was no one person's fault, but the injustice of the verdict acted as a catalyst for the tragic suicide that followed.

Helen replaced the items where she had found them knowing that the following day she would have to see to their safe disposal.

Bending down, she lifted the little bag from the floor and reached across the desk for the light switch. This time she could not avert her eyes from the photograph displayed in the silver frame that she had chosen so carefully all those years ago. There they were: the proud Detective Chief Inspector and his newly graduated daughter grinning unashamedly into the camera.

Helen turned out the light.

Some Other Love

SHE LAY ON HER BACK STARING up at the ceiling and listened to the even sound of his breathing. It was almost impossible not to resist the urge to join him in sleep but she forced her eyes to remain open and allowed her thoughts to drift back to a moment many years before when they were on their first official date.

She recalled the sun's descent over the horizon in a great splash of orange and red and the two of them lying side by side on their backs in the middle of a cornfield. They had talked innocently about their teenage dreams of the future and as the weak evening sun finally dwindled from sight he suddenly turned and kissed her full on the mouth. It was her first real taste of love.

She had been only fourteen then and he a year older but now, nearly thirty years on, she remembered the excitement of his touch that day and marvelled at how nothing had really changed. He still made her feel as though she was the only woman who really mattered in his life.

In the intervening years, of course, they had travelled very different roads and the excitement of that first love had become a distant memory to them both. After their schooldays were over he chose not to go to university and had instead set up a small transport company which was now a multi-million pound international business. She, on the other hand, had followed the advice of her parents and become a teacher. Their paths had never crossed again and the lives they led with their respective partners seemed, in the main at least, largely happy and fulfilled. Then a year ago, their destinies had once more collided.

She was in the local supermarket waiting rather impatiently at a checkout with her two children and as they began feeding the groceries on to the conveyor belt she glanced up to find him staring at her from a little way across the store.

After thirty years it was a shock to encounter him like that without warning and the sudden intake of air that she made was like breathing him in all over again after all those years. He seemed to have hardly changed at all except perhaps for the slight greying of his hair at the temples, but the boyish smile was still there as irresistible to her now as it had always been and she knew then that she was lost. It was not the most romantic place to start an affair but it was a catalyst for the awakening of emotions she had no idea she could still possess.

At first it was easy to excuse their illicit meetings as two old friends innocently catching up on lost time, but gradually they both realised that there was much more to it than that. They would meet more and more often, beginning to exchange little intimacies of their personal lives. He made her feel wanted and desired and her need for him seemed only to increase when they were apart.

That nice safe, predictable life of hers had changed irrevocably by a chance meeting in a supermarket and she seemed powerless to stop the destruction their liaisons might bring should they be discovered.

For his part, he was wracked with guilt for cheating on his wife who, after all, was not some kind of monster. In fact, he still felt love for her but any passion that had been between them in the past had somehow got lost in the world of babies, work and everyday life. Many of his associates, he knew, had their occasional indiscretions mainly during business trips abroad but it had never before occurred to him to be unfaithful or embark on an affair which made it all the more alarming when it happened.

The day he spotted his old girlfriend while he was out shopping heralded a fundamental change in how he viewed his life. What he had thought had been contentment in his marriage before, now felt like complacency. Otherwise how could he feel such utter joy in another woman's company? It was a question he could not answer and, in any case, refused now to confront. Neither of them could explain why it had happened, but they both knew that it was not some kind of sordid little affair where they made empty promises to each other.

They had agreed to give it a year after which it would have to be all or nothing. All or nothing. So cut and dry, she thought, as though it could possibly be as easy as that. As she felt him begin to stir next to her she turned on her side to watch him awakening from sleep. His eyes slowly opened and she saw the corners of his lovely mouth turn upwards into the saddest of smiles as he gently drew her towards him and they made love for the last time.

He had come to know every inch of her body and caressed her tenderly and with care, lingering just long enough in one place to feel her arousal before passing on. Afterwards they did not need to speak and he placed soft little kisses on her face where the rivulets of tears had begun to flow. She despised herself for her self-pity because their year together had been made up of gloriously happy times where crying had no role to play.

They parted silently at the station, neither of them being brave enough to say the words. As the train moved off she caught sight of him weaving his way amongst the crowds and then finally disappearing out of her life.

It was the right decision, she was sure of that. There was no doubt in her mind that she loved him just as she did her husband, albeit love of a very different kind. But what she needed was not simply the passion shared between two people enveloped in each others' arms in some anonymous hotel room, it was about arriving home after work and falling asleep on the sofa without anyone minding or looking like something the cat dragged in when she'd had a bad day. She knew that no matter what her lover had given her in the fantasy world they had created together it was never going to be enough and eventually one day they would both realise they had begun to lose the spark that had at first reunited them.

She knew this with certainty because that was how it was in the real world.

Suddenly, there was a call on her mobile and it was one of the children wondering when she would finally make it home. There was a homework that she needed help with and Daddy hadn't made the tea yet or washed any school shirts either. They all missed her and could she please hurry because Daddy was really hopeless without her and needed so much help.

As she put down the phone she began to will the train to move faster to its destination. She was going home for good and this time not out of some indignant sense of duty but because of what was waiting for her when she got there.

Perhaps it was not exciting, passionate or adventurous, but it was enough and as the dry, sepia cornfields of late summer rolled their way past the window of the train her eyes remained fixed ahead finally without the need for looking back.

Blasted Fridays

ONCE UPON A TIME, BUT NOT so very long ago, there was a troll called Wesley who lived quite happily beneath a bridge between two fields in a lush valley. For years he had fished in the river for his supper and enjoyed drinking the clear water that flowed down from the mountain stream above. No-one disturbed him and apart from the occasional courtesy call from a passing relative Wesley lived a quiet, non-eventful sort of life. That is, until they arrived.

One fine spring morning Wesley was having a well earned lie-in. The previous day he had been working hard on some minor repairs to his basement. It was a place he liked to retreat to every now and then because it was dark, slushy and cool - characteristics very soothing to a troll's soul. He had noticed recently that some little chinks of light were making their way through the caked mud that served as plaster between the stones and he had meticulously filled them in. For a troll, it was an exhausting but worthwhile task and Wesley felt that a job well done deserved a reward, hence his lie-in the following morning.

His huge saucer- like eyelids lay flatly closed against the wrinkled folds of his skin and in repose Wesley resembled some old toad that had recently been beaten up. But as trolls go, Wesley was actually extremely handsome. At sunrise his deep slumber was disturbed by an ungodly racket. TRIP TRAP, TRIP TRAP, TRIP TRAP. Something was walking across his ceiling.

I would dearly like to say that at this point Wesley leapt up and confronted the offending noisemaker with the brashness that has been attributed to him. However, at five in the morning he was not quite firing on all cylinders. Instead he sleepily raised his head above the railings and inquired politely, "Who, might I ask, is trip trapping over my roof at this very early hour of the day?"

"Mind your own business, you ugly troll," came the reply, as some whippersnapper of a goat looked him straight in the eye.

"Didn't your mother ever tell you that it's rude to say things like that?" said Wesley sheepishly.

"Oh, why don't you ask her yourself, you old fool," yapped the baby goat. "She's coming up right behind me." And with that poor old Wesley was dismissed with the flick of a tail and a disdainful glance.

Not surprisingly, mummy Billy Goat Gruff was following hot on the heels of her offspring. Wesley tried hard to think nice thoughts to himself, for he really wasn't a confrontational kind of guy and he waited patiently for Mrs Gruff to approach him.

"Good morning, Mrs Gruff," he said softly. "I see that your kid is availing himself of the beautiful lush grass on the other side of the bridge. Are you hoping to join him?"

Mrs Billy Goat Gruff looked at Wesley. Her eyes were the colour of amber and bulged menacingly from the sides of her head like two huge warts. Wesley found this oddly attractive but was acutely aware that they were not the kind of eyes you messed with on such a morning as this.

"Goats eat trolls," she growled threateningly, "especially when they poke their snouts into something that's none of their business." And with that she lifted her leg and smacked Wesley soundly on the forehead with her hoof. Then off she trotted over the bridge to join the kid.

Wesley had never encountered violence of any kind before. However, he had, many years ago, been the subject of cruel taunts by school children further down the valley which had led to his relocation to the isolated bridge. He felt sad that nobody had ever taken the time to know him or had made judgments about his personality because of his looks. But physical violence was something else and he lay stunned on the ground while a bump the size of a walnut emerged between his eyes.

The thumping in his temples was drowned out only by a distant rumble which was increasing in volume by the second and accompanied by a large cloud of grey dust. The perpetrator eventually came to a halt no more than six inches from Wesley's nose. Particles of grime danced in the morning sunlight floating casually through the slats of wood beneath and seeping silently into every nook and cranny of the home the house-proud troll had so painstakingly created. Something inside Wesley changed.

As the dust finally settled the source of this new intrusion made itself clear. The king of Billy Goats Gruff himself stood arrogant and conceited before our gentle troll and he turned the points of two finely honed horns in Wesley's direction.

"One more word of insolence out of you and you're dead," he bellowed, stamping his feet on the ground and no doubt causing even more disorder to the dwelling below.

Wesley shrugged. "Fine by me," he said. "I was only meaning to pass the time of day with you all and meant you no offence, Sir Gruff. Please be my guest and pass over my bridge at your leisure."

The goat was baffled. He had thought that, at the very least, the stupid troll would be spoiling for a fight and that he could prove his dominance over him by mauling Wesley and throwing his body into the river. Then everyone in the valley would see King Billy Goat Gruff for what he was - a clever, underestimated animal who was not intimidated by a grotesque, deformed little creature who lived under a bridge. But he could hardly kill someone who had not put up any kind of a fight. So to save face he decided to proceed haughtily to the other side to join the rest of his family. Satisfaction could be sought another day.

Wesley watched as the three goats made their way across the field towards the greenest stretch of pasture. He wondered if he should tell them. Certainly a few moments ago it had been on the tip of his tongue, but then they had all been so terribly rude to him which had hurt his feelings. Perhaps he might have excused the bad manners or even wavered a common assault charge against Mrs

Gruff, but messing up his house was a different matter. He didn't have to look to know the chaos that awaited him when he re-entered his den and that made him very angry after all those hours of housekeeping he had put in.

Just then, from down in the foothills of the valley, came the toll of the church bells.

CLANG. CLANG. CLANG. Three chimes down and seven to go.

Just enough time for Wesley to slide through the special trap door he had designed especially for moments such as these and disappear into the safety of the depths below.

Only last week his uncle had called to warn him of the imminent arrival of the quarry blasters who would be working for several weeks high up in the mountain.

"Watch out for Friday," cautioned his uncle. "That's the day they will be exploding the main fall of rocks which are sure to tumble in your direction. The church bells will ring out ten times to allow everyone to get to safety."

Wesley thought about this as he heard the tenth bell toll. He was secure and protected down in his basement but could feel the first tremor of the explosions as the rocks above began to shudder and crack. He slept for twelve hours on the trot.

A few weeks later a beautiful troll was sent to deal with his compensation claim for post traumatic stress syndrome, and as in all good stories, they fell head over heels in love. Now, on a pleasant spring day, they can be seen playing with the baby trollets on the lush green grass outside their home (now extensively renovated, of course). Occasionally one of the children will ask, "Papa, tell us the story of how we got those troll knolls in our garden."

On such moments you will see a strange glint in Wesley's eye and he will smile knowingly as he turns to inspect his immaculate home - not a speck of dust in sight.

Safe in Your Mouth

IT WAS AN ENIGMA. GEORGE HAD never indicated who she was or why he had kept the photograph for all those years, but her face continued to smile from the tatty frame beside his bed and shed its warmth on all who looked upon it. Whether it was senility or simply a reluctance to share his memories no one could tell. In fact, nobody even bothered to ask anymore for George had disappeared a long time ago into some impenetrable world they could not reach.

Today he was folded like an origami bird into his favourite chair while music hummed softly somewhere along the corridor. Then across the airwaves of some forgotten wasteland they were playing that song. George's eyelids sputtered and for one glorious moment he was back in the dance hall looking into a pair of smiling green eyes and leading her out on to the floor.

The band was playing the Tennessee Waltz, his favourite, and he shyly placed one palm on her waist while the other cupped fingers as delicate as daisy petals.

Together they glided over the parquet, stepping easily to the waltz beat, their eyes pupil to pupil, unblinking. She was lovely. Not beautiful, but lovely, and he was happy with that. Her curls, the colour of new autumn, flowed over her shoulders as she moved and the full yellow skirt she wore swished about her legs like sunshine. When the music stopped they stood self-consciously in each other's company, neither of them wanting to be the first to move away. Typically it was Nora who broke the silence.

"So, George Dawson," she said, "you're not going to arrest me then?" A hand was placed coquettishly on one hip and her head dipped sideways teasing him.

"Next time I catch you without a light on that bike of yours I just might," George laughed, leading her quickly back on to the dance floor as the band started up its next set.

They had encountered each other earlier on in the day when he was about to come off duty. His sergeant had sent him to check out some dubious activities at an old poteen still and he had been returning to clock off when she almost mowed him over on her bike.

"Sorry officer," she shouted but carried on peddling, hair and clothing flapping their nonchalance into George's smitten face. Back at the station he made discreet enquiries.

"Must have been one of those Baker girls," said the sarge, who knew everyone worthy of knowing in the district. "Nora, probably, the youngest; she was off across the water for a while helping with the war effort but now I hear she's at the doctor's place helping out."

When he returned home George carefully laid out his uniform on the bed. His boots still shone from the spit and polish he had performed on them that same morning for he had a great sense of pride in his police livery. He did, in fact, look terribly handsome in his uniform, a fact that had not gone unnoticed as Nora Baker sped past him on her bike earlier, but he was not to know that then, of course. Only later at the dance did George sense that she might like him and that was enough.

They started walking out together and George never questioned her affection for him, but one day through his shyness he was minded to ask, "Nora, what do you think love means?"

Her reply came as effortlessly as water from the spring well.

"Oh George," she whispered, "when someone loves you, the way they say your name is different. You know that your name feels safe in their mouth – like you and me."

Afterwards came word of George's unexpected promotion; a bigger station, more opportunities to further his career but in the city, seventy miles away. Nora made it easy for him.

"You must go, George," she told him. "You'll come back for me, I know, and I'll be here waiting."

She never doubted it and George himself was at first full of great intentions. He sent letters with talk of the great ballrooms he had visited and the wonderful sights he had seen in his new exciting world. She in turn replied with words of her affection but although she waited patiently for him he never came.

George's heart had been stolen, not by some interloping lover, but by a far more powerful adversary, the buzz and hum of urban life.

Nora carried on waiting for George's return refusing to admit that he might have abandoned her to spinsterhood. Long after she had ceased to write him letters she continued to hope that he had not forgotten her and that one day they would eventually be reunited. Through the passage of years she saw her friends become parents and eventually, grandparents, but still Nora carried on believing.

Today, then, she sits in her wheelchair, her body wracked by the frailties of old age but content to have been assigned a room with a pleasant view overlooking the garden.

A care worker is unpacking her small case and placing the folded belongings carefully onto the bed.

"Well, Nora," she says kindly, "let's get you settled into your new home. I'll play that record you've brought with you if you like".

And as the stylus rests in its familiar groove the crackle of a Tennessee Waltz echoes the memory of years down along the corridor.

First Day at School

IT WAS MY FIRST DAY AT PRIMARY school and my mother clasped my hand in hers and held it tightly. I wore the coat she so lovingly made for me from an old blanket and grimaced when the hairiness of it irritated my skin. Shafts of sunlight floated through the scullery window and I wondered at the necessity of a coat on such a fine day, but outside the wind bit at my knees and I was suddenly thankful for the blanket coat to keep me warm.

The school wasn't far away and I watched my brother and sister shuffle begrudgingly ahead of us; my brother's back was stiff and slouched as though he carried a heavy weight. He hated school and I wondered what could be so terrible about a place to make him feel like that.

We crossed the road and marched over the common where the men from the council had made their final cut the day before – there would be no more grass houses to build until the spring.

Our family band was now expanding as others joined us on the journey and my sister, with her skinny legs and slight frame, marched out in front. I was aware that she was thinking about her new teacher because she'd whispered her anxieties into my ear in bed the night before.

We reached the school gates with their towering stone pillars on either side and walked beneath a wrought iron sign declaring, "Hart Memorial Primary School". It was as though a magic switch was flicked on inside me and my stomach tightened with knots of excitement and expectation. A lady with a kindly face stood at the big door and she said something to my mother and then smiled at me. We followed her into the warmth of the building and I was suddenly aware that my older siblings had gone – it was scary that they should just disappear like that without me even noticing.

My mother released my hand and pulled the straps of the satchel from my shoulders, gently withdrawing a small wash bag with 'Lynda' smartly sewn across one side. She lifted me so that I could loop the drawstring over a cloakroom peg and I fleetingly caught the scent of apple and soap from inside. It was reassuring, smothered as it was by other less familiar aromas emanating from further down the corridor. Then without warning the shrillness of a morning bell rang out to signal the beginning of a school day and the crushing reality of separation from my mother abruptly hit me. I watched as she hurried away, willing her to turn around with every step, until finally she disappeared from view.

Standing then in the cloakroom, I looked at all the other coats on pegs, the wash bags with their names, now hanging there beside my own. 'Louise' and 'Jennifer', 'Alan', 'Dan' and 'Paul'. Their owners stood around me, motherless and scared, like me. I bit my lip but couldn't halt the trembling of my chin when I heard the first whimper. And surrounded by a sea of equally bewildered faces I waited for instructions as the great crescendo of tears began to echo their way through the big doors and out searchingly into an empty playground.

The Birthday Lunch

SHE WAS WAITING FOR ME, SITTING at a picnic table in the dappled shade of a silver birch, its leaves delicately coloured the new green of spring that we'd both come to value and love. Gravel crackled and scrunched beneath the soles of my shoes as I walked the final few yards along the path to meet her and I could feel the first real warmth of a May sun seeping through my jacket and deep into my back. It was a fine day to have a birthday. Hers and mine. It was the last one that we would spend together.

I gave her a hug, feeling the genuine affection of friendship reciprocated in her embrace and then we sat down together in the sunshine to have our lunch. She produced hers from her handbag, a packet of macro-biotic soup as unappetising as the cup of boiling water she added it to. I ordered, and ate, the house special.

We exchanged gifts, laughing because we had inadvertently bought one another the same thing; a single photo frame holding a picture of us at some charity event. And after the laughter, we talked. We talked of forbidden things. Cancer. Death. And about how we'd like people to remember us after we died.

'Plant a forest flame for me,' she said, her voice shaky and unsure with the finality of it. So I promised I would - it was easy then to agree to the ridiculous.

She drank her soup. It smelled of dying teabags hung to dry and I chided her for such self-sacrifice. In the still air of the garden we shared our birthday as we had in years gone by and we also shared our disease. Children played innocently in a nearby park, their laughter bouncing off the trees like little leaves of truth finally falling at our feet. Souvenirs of life. Reminders of our own mortality. And as the gathering clouds collected to occlude the sun, we rose to leave.

'Same time next year then,' she said, collecting together her things and giving me one last embrace. Her eyes were suddenly blazing in defiance as she spoke but I saw beneath the bravado her vulnerability and her fear and I could no longer look her in the eye.

I stood and watched as she drove off, the tyres of her car screeching on the tarmac as she went, her voice through the open window shouting words that were sucked up and obliterated by the breeze.

I waited until she was out of sight before returning to the table. A waiter had already come to clear away the things and there was little evidence of our having been for lunch at all yet somehow it seemed right to feel her presence there for one last time.

I thought of other birthdays still to come when the forest flame in my garden would open up its fiery blossoms to the spring sunshine.

May the second. As good a day as any I suppose, to celebrate somebody's birthday.

Gettin' Hitched

THE PHONE RANG AT NINE O' CLOCK. "Fifteen," drawled an unfamiliar voice at the end of the line. "If you make it here in fifteen minutes he'll try to fit you in." We were there in less than ten.

'Payne County Courthouse, Stillwater,' read the sign above the entrance and inside men wearing Stetsons scurried about in sharp designer suits - nobody batted an eye. This was, after all, Oklahoma, the Sooner State - cowboy country.

"Getting' hitched?" enquired the man on reception when we asked for directions. "Down that corridor, turn left. But you'd better make it fast y'all."

And off we went to get hitched wondering why, in what was probably the most laid back state in the US, everyone should suddenly be in such an almighty hurry.

The room was hard to miss. Enormous brass handles and bold gold letters on the door told us that 'Judge Ray Lee Wall' resided there and we entered a scene reminiscent of the set on Bonanza.

A shotgun hung ostentatiously over an elaborate stone fireplace, its shaft shiny and smooth from years of snuggling easily under a hunter's armpit and as if to prove a point, several of its apparent victims, stuffed and unseeing, stared out at us from their final resting place up on the wall. Judge Ray Lee Wall was clearly a man of some endeavour over and above his legal skills.

165

The delicate perfume of summer jasmine wafted through open windows to compete with harsher more consuming scents of buckskin and cigar smoke. A clock ticked. Typewriter keys connected to rapid fingers in the adjoining room and there, propped up in a corner looking rather lonely and out of place, was the source of our demise; a fishing rod. The realisation that our nuptials were to be usurped by a fishing expedition was finally beginning to sink in. Then, like the dust that blows its way across an Oklahoma Plain, the great Judge Wall himself made his entrance.

At first I was too stunned to speak. I had half expected a gowned version of Perry Mason and instead got Indiana Jones meets Clint Eastwood.

"Ready?" he boomed and the ceremony began. Witnesses were sought: a secretary, a courthouse clerk, the two closest people available at the time.

We got hitched in five minutes flat – something of a record we were told later. A clock was chiming the half hour as Judge Ray Lee Wall extended a hand in congratulations, and grabbing his rod with the other departed on a fishing trip he, at least, has probably long since forgotten.

We picked up the marriage certificate and made our way back to the car park and our faithful rusty old Ford Galaxy. My newly hitched husband started up the engine and we sputtered and heaved towards the expressway that would lead us unwittingly into the oncoming path of Hurricane Elisha.

But that, as they say, is another story.

Hush-a-bye Baby

THE PAIN IS NIGGLING AT FIRST. It nudges its way from the pit of my stomach to somewhere near the small of my back. I'm thirteen weeks pregnant and it doesn't take much to know that something is not the way it ought to be. So the doctor comes.

She's strange to me for we've only recently arrived in the neighbourhood but still she's nice and she breathes on her fingers to warm them before examining me. It's a thoughtful gesture I appreciate more than she knows.

Her face is impassive when she breaks the news, but I need her honesty; truth being somehow more believable when surrounded by the familiar. And anyway, I need to prepare myself before we leave home.

The plastic doors swing closed behind us with a loud slap. It's a very hospital sound – a reminder of this place I've come to that will be my world for the next twenty-four hours. The place where I know now with certainty that I will lose my baby; I understand this, I do. But I'm not yet ready to believe it.

The nurses are already waiting and they lead the way to a small side room off the main ward. The bed has crisp white sheets and there's an underlying smell of disinfectant but it's private and I'm grateful for that.

My husband, who's come along with me, is told politely, "There's nothing you can do but let nature take its course. Come back and collect your wife in the morning." Don't they know that

167

it's his baby too? Don't they even think about that? But I'm left alone to wait.

I lie down on top of the bed and stare at four white walls and a sink. The truth is I want to be by myself – to share nothing but my own space and to selfishly breathe in my own air. So I let the hospital silence settle over me and ask my questions to an empty room.

What colour would my baby's eyes have been? The colour of his hair? Her hair? And will the sense of loss I feel ever really disappear?

Later, when it's over, the doctors tell me that it's just been nature's way; that it happens to women every day and I'll have another child to replace the one I've lost. As if it's as easy as that I think, watching their white coats recede through the doorway. As if it's as easy as that.

I hear soft footfall in the corridor outside. One of the nurses has forgotten something, I suppose. She comes in quietly and sits with me on the bed.There is a look of undisguised compassion on her face.

Without warning she takes my hand in hers and squeezes it tightly for a moment.

"It's okay Lynda," she whispers. "Time will help it heal, you'll see."

This simple act of kindness from a stranger is something that I'll not forget. The relief I feel from her words is overwhelming.

My healing has a long way still to go, but it's a start.

Little Shrew

I HADN'T NOTICED IT. It was hiding underneath the car, its tiny form camouflaged perfectly among the gravel as my daughter moved off down the driveway. Our collie Meg, on the other hand, was rather more astute, and in one pounce she had it in her mouth – a little shrew.

I couldn't bring myself to blame the dog. No malice was involved in this playful display of normal canine behaviour, but as I extricated the tiny insectivore from its confinement I knew the damage had already been done.

It curled itself up into the centre of my palm – a funny mouse-like thing with velvety fur and a pointy little snout, and a tail like the end of one of those red liquorice laces you used to buy in the sweetie shop.

I saw its tummy blowing in and out. I saw that its breath came laboured and erratic from its mouth. But most of all I saw that its eyes were open, and they were staring up at me - in what? Fear? Expectation? Truly, looking back, I'm not exactly sure which one it was myself.

It was a lovely afternoon. Leaves had gathered in pockets at the side of the lawn, so I fashioned a makeshift nest amongst the dry foliage and very carefully placed the tiny shrew in its midst. Still its eyes refused to close. Shock., I thought. Perhaps it's nothing more than that after all. Surely it would revive. It would survive.

I covered it with a big leaf and left it there for a while – to see. When I returned I saw that its eyes had finally succumbed to the light but it was still alive, panting heavily, and clearly in some pain. What could I do but end its misery?

Feeling like an executioner, I went to the house and returned with a wad of cotton wool. I had never wilfully killed an animal before and something about even considering it made me feel nauseous, but I knew it needed to be done.

Holding the cotton wool over its nose, I felt the shrew twitch and its legs jerk before I stopped. I couldn't do it. It just wasn't in me to do it. So finally I left it there among the leaves, I knew, to die. 'Coward' I accused myself, walking away.

All through the night I prayed to be forgiven for my weakness. As the first fingers of light stretched across the garden I went to check. The hedges were full of singing - nature does not defer to the demise of a tiny mammal. When I reached the place where my shrew had been I saw that it had gone, and save for the twitch of a leaf on dry earth, nothing stirred.

Of course, I'd like to think that it survived, and even now is foraging for food among the leaf litter in my garden. But I know it probably perished, consumed by some creature destined to assuage my guilt for a deed I could not do myself.

And all must now be well. For nature, surely, gives back what she takes.

One Day in January

THIS IS NO ORDINARY DAY, I THINK. The morning sun blinks out from a January sky and there are things to do that I have always done, but still I know that this day will probably change my life.

I get the children ready. They chuckle at a cartoon on TV and wriggle themselves reluctantly into their coats. I am trying to keep everything normal.

I take my son to nursery and my daughter to school. They are very young. Only three and five. I have arranged for them to be picked up later - in case.

I arrive home to wait. My husband works overseas so I must ask for favours from friends, and today I need a lift. There is an appointment at ten. The phone rings. My friend's car has broken down. Can I get someone else? Yes, I say, and phone another friend – a man – to see if he can help. I tell him we'll be back by twelve.

The hospital smells bleached and new; you can almost taste it on your tongue. We are directed to a corridor where women sit and I feel for my companion who has suddenly been thrust among this alien female world. We talk easily together until a nurse appears and hesitantly attempts my name. I smile in recognition and she leads me to a room where I undress. The wound has not yet healed on my left breast but I know the procedure and lie down expectantly on the bed.

He arrives in five minutes. A doctor whom I haven't seen before. He holds my notes in his hands - my life in his hands. And he says, "You have a malignancy in your breast. If you get dressed we'll discuss treatment."

He leaves and waits in the adjacent room while I begin to put my clothes back on. Slowly. For I need time to think. What about the kids? My husband? My friend who remains unsuspectingly outside? My feet take me to the other room.

"Right," I announce. "Tell me what this means."

I sound like an idiot. I know already what it means; I just want him to tell me what I want to hear, not what I already know.

I think of my friend in the corridor - waiting. I feel sorrier for him than I do for myself – this is not what he signed up for this morning after all.

When I see him I say,"Sorry, but we'll be here rather longer than I thought."

He touches my arm - a gesture that says more than a thousand empty words.

It is dark when we leave. My children have been taken to a school friend's house but I ask my male companion to take me directly home. To prepare. I don't need the company of anyone else right now.

He drops me at my gate and I walk the final few yards to the backdoor. I turn the key in the lock and pause a second before entering the empty house. The phone is ringing.

My husband?

My mum?

The door clicks quietly into place behind me as I reach out to pick up the receiver.

Photo Booth

I MADE A RECE OF THE LOCATION some days earlier as nothing in my mission could be left to chance. There it stood, tucked anonymously away in a corner of our local supermarket looking rather lonely and dejected but fitting perfectly into my requirements. It seemed like just the place to have a passport photograph taken for our upcoming trip to Iran.

It was a Sunday, quite late on in order to avoid the main influx of customers and I arrived armed with the necessary accoutrements for my task. Four 'pound' coins. Lip gloss. A silk scarf cheerfully patterned blue and white. No one could say I hadn't come prepared.

It seemed to be waiting for me; the photo booth. A lady with perfect teeth, in fact four sets of perfect teeth, smiled out from a row of identical images along one side. A mirror, one of those out of focus squidgy ones, was juxtaposed beside her suggesting 'you too could look like this'. I checked my own squidgy reflection, applied a dab of gloss and checked my change; enough to cover one attempt. No room for error then, and in I went.

A photo booth, I soon discovered, is not a tardis. Holding my belongings gingerly in one hand I began my preparations. 'Before entering payment please adjust the seat to your height' read instruction number one. Easy enough you might think, so I swivelled the seat. And swivelled. But the seat had long since refused any form of proper rotation and remained stubbornly at the same height. Fine if you've got very short legs and a long neck, I thought, eventually managing to press my back hard against the wall and, bearing my weight on my knees, strained to get the proper height.

Even then I could tell that my head was not correctly inside the eggy shape that had mysteriously appeared in the screen before me. I still hadn't put on the scarf. Never mind.

Instruction number two. Enter money and choose a pose you like before pressing the green button. Right, it was time to don the scarf. I wrapped it round my head and beamed idiotically into the camera. Nothing happened. Then I remembered I hadn't put in the money.

It's hard to enter coins in a slot, push a button and strike a happy pose when your legs have gone into spasm beneath you, and the flash got me as I began to slide down the wall. But by then I was beyond caring. I gathered my things and stayed put. No way was I waiting outside in full view of the public after that ordeal.

When I eventually heard the drone of the developer squeezing out my image I grabbed the photos and ran.

Some time later we entered Iran through Tehran airport and I handed over my passport to the waiting official. I watched as he carefully examined the photograph of a wild-eyed Irish woman with a demented stare and decidedly lopsided head gear. Then, turning to me with some concern, he asked, "So, Mrs Tavakoli, in your country is it forbidden for women to smile?"

Next time I'm going to the chemist.

Say a Little Prayer

YOU WERE WANDERING IN THE MIDDLE of the road, misplaced like a vulnerable child on the first day of school, and I almost ran you over - it was too dangerous a place for me to stop. My eyes searched the rear view mirror for your image but it was gone, obscured by the sea of morning traffic coming from behind. It was as though you had never been at all.

I dropped my son at school and began the final stage of my journey to work. There would be time enough to stop at the newsagents to buy a paper. I pulled in and parked and when I looked up there you were again, on the footpath beside my car. You reminded me of my dad.

"Are you okay?" I asked, conscious that I was invading your space - startling you with the question.

"Thank you. Yes," you said. But you weren't. I could see very well that you weren't.

We walked in unison for a few yards as far as the lights. I noticed the clean crease down the front of your twill trousers. You wore dapper brown brogues on your feet. And I wondered if anyone was missing you yet.

The pedestrian light was red but still you carried on, the destination inside your head precluding any normal line of thought. So I went with you, fearful for your safety yet reticent to cross the boundary keeping the lives of strangers like us apart. Then you were stumbling; falling in slow motion towards the concrete, and landing sprawled in an undignified heap upon the road. A man at the bus stop helped me lead you safely to the footpath. Your glasses tottered on the end of your nose, your mouth was agape with the shock of it but I could see your pride had taken the brunt of the damage.

"Can I call someone to come for you?" I asked fixing the glasses horizontal again. Your eyes were the colour of a May sky. They looked at me as if I wasn't there.

I tried again, "Come into the shop," I said, this time grasping your frail fingers with my own, "and you can sit down and have a drink." But you shook you head, adamant to be once more on your way.

"You can't force him into it, love," advised the man from the bus stop, so I reluctantly let you go, watching you shuffle your way along the street, shoulders bent, head cocked slightly to one side. And I watched until, like the speck on an old black and white television set, you vanished into nothingness.

I carried on to work, overcome by the burden of guilt that suddenly clung to me like a shroud. Somewhere in the distance a siren stung the morning stillness and I said a hasty prayer for someone in need I didn't know. Somebody perhaps whose name I never asked.

And all I knew was you reminded me of my dad.

The Burial

SHE WAS ALREADY STIFF WHEN I found her lying dumped beside a ditch not twenty yards from my home, her beautiful white fur marred only by a spot of red at the temples, those unforgettable green eyes forever shut to the living world.

I got a sheet from the house to wrap her in and pleated it round her carefully so that she was safe and wouldn't fall out. Her corpse was surprisingly heavy for a cat but I did not want any help and would tell the children later in my own time.

They say that when something dies a part of you goes too and I believe it. I believe it when I see any dead animal on the road. And I say a little prayer. I doubt the person who ran her over feels the same.

She wasn't even ours. She just started to appear at our back door and of course we fed and watered her. A white cat with green eyes, skinny and bedraggled; none of us could resist. It began with titbits now and again but inevitably there were tins of cat food and a little bed made for her in the empty stable. Fatter and fatter she became. Well rounded, healthy. And, of course, finally, pregnant.

She had her kittens on the back doorstep. Four tiny rats before she licked them dry and let them suckle at her fat belly. When it was time, we moved them to the warmth of the stable and left her to it. She was a good mum and I am sure she missed her kittens when they were finally found homes some time later. I don't know if she ever really forgave me for it.

We had her spayed. A stray cat, not even ours - fifty pounds. But necessary.

Her fur had only just begun to cover her scar when she was killed. I had been thinking how close she was again to being perfect.

I told the children after lunch and let them see her one last time. And then I got a spade and dug a hole. I dug it very deep and thought of nothing save the brown earth and the red on white of her bloody temple.

When I began to cry I do not know. I think it was when I finished the hole. I know I stood there sobbing for perhaps half an hour and I let it happen as I knew I must. Tears for a cat. Tears for a friend. Tears for three friends. At their funerals I could not cry my uncontrollable tears for them. So I stood, only me there in the garden, burying my cat and so much more.

I marked the grave with a cross and covered it with stones. Only later did my daughter come and, standing with me, say her childlike prayer of thanks.

Dear God,

Thanks for giving us Whitey. She made us happy and she made me smile. She gave us lots of nice things and made us feel good. Please look after her.

Amen.

And Amen to all that.

Two Minute Timer

I WAS METICULOUSLY MARKED OUT WITH a pen seven days before; every black line and dot carefully applied to my left breast with precision accuracy.

"Be sure that you don't get it wet," they warned, "It'll have to stay there for the next six weeks."

I knew my children would have something to say about that, and they did. "Mummy got her booby written on," remarked my daughter without taking much of an interest.

"Mummy got big tattoo!" exclaimed my son gleefully, immediately poking my breast with a chubby little finger. After that neither of them mentioned it much again.

The nurses gave me a blue robe to put on while I was waiting to go in for treatment. It reminded me of the chalet maid's uniform I wore at Butlins one summer when I was a student, so I had to laugh. Memories of a misspent youth, but it helped to take my mind off other things before I went in.

The machinery was big, clinical and cold. Intimidating. But mostly big, and I was glad I'd been forewarned. A doctor came to speak to me while I was lying down; vulnerable – bare flesh exposed beneath the huge Goliath machine above and I wanted to sit up, converse with him on equal terms while fully clothed, but I couldn't. He checked my marks and told me that I shouldn't move in any way while the machine was on, for six whole weeks, for two whole minutes every time.

179

"What if I sneeze?" I inquired, but he laughed and said with the authority of one who knows, "Nobody ever sneezes." And he left.

Bzzzzzzz went a buzzer as the doors sucked shut and an orange light above, ignited. My eyes closed. Ummmm hummed Goliath as he began to launch his attack. Battle had commenced.

Against the soft drone of the machine there was only silence and the noiseless clock inside my head that counted out the seconds of the timer I'd been set. Two minutes. One hundred and twenty seconds. No taste. No touch. No smell or sight. Just the constant hum that marked the death knell of an enemy within.

And I finally began to let go, to feel enveloped by the radiation's gift of healing in my breast. I felt the power of it. Dangerous. Frightening. But ultimately the giver of a cancer patient's precious need – of hope.

One hundred and eighteen. One hundred and nineteen. One hundred and... buzzzzzz. Green light on. Doors opening. Voices. Normality. Time stops for no man, isn't that what they say? And life does go on even if you've got cancer.

Within the sanctuary of my cubicle I donned the clothes I came in and prayed to the God of radiation to make me well. Then somewhere in the distance I could hear another buzzer sounding - someone else's private battle had commenced. I made my journey home.

Six weeks. I thought. A tiny price to pay.

And I never, ever sneezed.

Bazaar

THE PORTAL TO ESFAHAN'S ANCIENT BAZAAR allows respite from the Persian sun and I pause for a moment to watch my children walking together up ahead. They are curiously untroubled by the glances they attract by their paler complexions and European appearance.

"Yallah maman, zud boch!" calls my daughter Farah practising her Farsi, "Come on mum, hurry up!" So I take my husband's hand and like Ali Baba entering the magic cave in the mountainside, step into a twenty-first century treasure trove of my own.

The call for prayer echoes from distant minarets and sunlight bounces off the cobbles that lead a path through the myriad of shops. All day I've been searching for some special gifts for the folks back home and now I'm running out of time. There is only an hour left before we have to leave.

Just when I have almost given up I see the answer to my prayers – a stall of intricately patterned tablecloths in every shape and hue. Perfect. This is definitely it, I think.

A young boy appears and sensing my interest announces in broken English, "Come see factory! Many more beautiful cloths for you there."

I look at my husband. "A factory?" I query silently with my eyes. How can we have time to visit somebody's factory?

But our enticer is adamant, "Very near," he invites again.

And, of course, the proposition is too intriguing for us to refuse. So we follow him through the snaked passageways until after only a short time he stops and with a flourish of arms directs us through a doorway and into a small half lit room.

"Factory!" he announces with pride.

Sitting lotus - positioned in the middle of the floor is an old man. He has a wooden template strapped to his forearm and he is stamping out patterns on to a cloth with red dye. Tablecloths are piled up in hillocks around the walls – some complete, some unfinished but all tenderly created by the one - man factory sitting there in front of us.

"How long," I inquire, "have you been making these?"

He glances up. "Pan - jâh sâl," he says simply. Fifty years. And he smoothes the fabric out with loving hands and works until the pattern comes alive again beneath his touch.

I buy a dozen or so cloths but my delight at their discovery has been dampened suddenly by the simple dignity of one old man. As we leave he thanks us for our custom and for honouring his humble factory with our presence. I cannot bring myself to tell him that the value of one cloth is no more than a pack of cigarettes back home.

Outside the chatter of trade and barter continues to resonate through the labyrinth of streets while the sun maintains its vigil in a blue Iranian sky.

With a heavy heart I gather up my precious purchases and take my leave.

About the author

Lynda Tavakoli, author of two novels, 'Attachment' and 'Of Broken Things', lives near Lisburn, County Down in Northen Ireland.

Her poetry and prose have been broadcast on both BBC Radio Ulster and RTE Sunday Miscellany.

Literary successes include poetry and short story prizes at Listowel, the Mencap short story competition and the Mail on Sunday novel competition.

Lynda's work has been included in a wide variety of publications including Templar Poets' Anthology Skein, Abridged (Absence/Magnolia/Silence/Primal/Mara), The Incubator Journal, Panning for Poems, Circle and Square, CAP anthologies, North West Words, Four X Four (Poetry NI), Live Encounters magazine, The Honest Ulsterman and A New Ulster.

She was selected as The Irish Times Hennessy poet of the month in October 2015 for her poems about dementia, a recurring theme in both her poetry and prose.

Lynda has facilitated literary recitals at a number of Northern Ireland libraries and edited the prose and poetry anthology 'Linen' for the Irish Linen Museum.

This is her first collection of short stories.

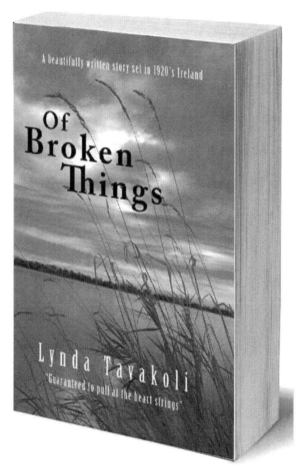

It is 1920's Ireland and John Flynn is ten years old when his much longed for sister Stela is born at their isolated cottage. She is a beautiful child whom John sees as a gift sent to alleviate the harshness of his life with an alcoholic father Redmond.

Within a few weeks of Stela's arrival John is unexpectedly left to look after his mother and sister during a snowstorm after Redmond fails to return from one of his many prolonged absences. Stela grows strong under the protection and deep love of her brother but when she approaches her third birthday she inexplicably withdraws from the world. Unforeseen tragedy follows and slowly a web of deceit begins to unravel.

This is a story of divided loyalties and deception, of fear and mistrust, but also one of love and joy that will pull at the heartstrings until the very last page.

17853101R00110

Printed in Poland
by Amazon Fulfillment
Poland Sp. z o.o., Wrocław